Grandma's Magical Storybook

This book belongs to:

_____

_____

Grandma's
Magical
Storybook

PaRRagon

Bath · New York · Singapore · Hong Kong · Cologne · Delhi
Melbourne · Amsterdam · Johannesburg · Shenzhen

This edition published by Parragon in 2012
Parragon
Queen Street House
4 Queen Street
Bath BA1 1HE, UK
www.parragon.com

ISBN 978-1-4454-9100-4

Printed in China

Contents

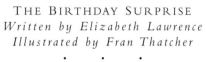

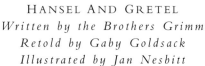

Gran's Magic Wardrobe

Jenna's Gran wasn't like other grans. She didn't come visiting very often and she never, ever baked cookies or knitted colourful jumpers. Not ever!

You see, Jenna's gran was an explorer. She was always off visiting some faraway corner of the world. So she didn't have time for visiting and baking like ordinary grans. But Jenna didn't care. She thought her gran was just brilliant. When she did come to stay, she always gave Jenna the most fantastic presents and she always told the best stories about her adventures.

8

So, you can imagine how excited Jenna was when Gran came to stay for the summer. She couldn't wait to see what wonderful things Gran had brought back with her this time.

But the only thing Gran brought was the biggest, ugliest wardrobe Jenna had ever seen.

"You don't mind me storing it in here, do you?" Gran asked, as it was pushed into Jenna's tiny bedroom.

"But why do you need such a big wardrobe?" asked Jenna.

"Ah, well, things aren't always what they seem," winked Gran. But Jenna wasn't really listening. She was busy thinking how ugly the wardrobe made her room look.

Jenna lay glaring at the wardrobe while Gran told her a bedtime story.

"…and that's how I stopped the Tikuti Tribe from burning the wardrobe," finished Gran. But, for once, Jenna wasn't listening to Gran. In fact, Jenna wasn't very happy.

9

Gran had forgotten to bring her a present. To make matters worse, she'd cluttered up Jenna's beautiful bedroom with her horrible wardrobe. It wasn't even as if Gran had that many clothes.

The next morning, a letter arrived for Gran.

"Fantastic," she said after reading it. "I've been invited to lead an expedition up the Katani River. The only thing is, I have to leave today."

Jenna was very sorry to wave her Gran goodbye and she was even more sorry that she didn't take her horrid wardrobe with her.

That night, after Jenna had said goodnight to Mum and Dad, she sat on her bed staring at the wardrobe. Why did Gran want such an ugly thing? What did she keep in it?

Jenna was sure that Gran wouldn't mind if she took a quick peep. She slipped from the bed and tiptoed over to the wardrobe. Before she even touched it, the door swung open. A soft breeze seemed to come from the wardrobe. Jenna crept closer. Hmm, it smelled lovely – just like a forest.

Jenna stepped in and pushed past one of Gran's old raincoats.

Suddenly, she felt herself falling. She closed her eyes and waited for the bump. But she landed on something soft. When she opened her eyes, she blinked twice then pinched herself. She must be dreaming.

She was no longer inside Gran's wardrobe. Instead, she seemed to be in a beautiful, sunny forest.

"Hiya, Jenna," said a voice. "We've been expecting you."

Jenna looked up and was surprised to find herself being spoken to by a colourful bird.

"B…b…but where am I?" whispered Jenna, feeling just the tiniest bit afraid.

"You're in The Wardrobe," chirped another voice. Jenna looked around to find that it belonged to another bird. "Gran told us that you'd be popping in," he continued.

"B…b…but birds don't talk," stuttered Jenna.

"In The Wardrobe everything speaks," said a tree, helping Jenna to her feet. "That's just the way things are."

11

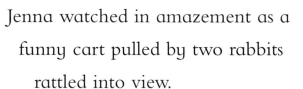

Just then, Jenna heard the toot of a horn.

"Look smart," cried the tree. "His

nibs is coming."

Jenna watched in amazement as a

funny cart pulled by two rabbits

rattled into view.

"Welcome, welcome," cried a

voice and out jumped a little man.

The funniest little man Jenna had

ever seen. He was no bigger than Jenna was

but his head was just enormous and on it he wore what looked like a

dustbin.

"Ah, I see you're admiring my crown,"

smiled the funny little man. "It blew in

from The World Outside one

day. Isn't it the finest crown

you've ever seen?"

Jenna tried very hard not to laugh.

"Anyway, allow me to introduce

myself. I am Tootiturtletoof, the king of

The Wardrobe. But my friends call me

Toot for short."

He shook Jenna's hand so hard

that her feet almost left the ground.

"As granddaughter of Gran the Great, who saved The Wardrobe from being burnt at the hands of the Tikuti Tribe, you are an honoured guest here. As it's not every day that we have honoured guests, we're going to have a party."

Toot clapped his hands and the wood jumped into action. Trees shook their branches, so that fruit and nuts fell onto plates below. Birds dropped berries from the sky. Chattering creatures, carrying trays of cakes and sandwiches, appeared out of nowhere. Other creatures danced around decorating the place with colourful flowers and leaves, and jugs of sparkling drink appeared out of thin air.

"Let the party begin," cried Toot and a band of squirrels started to play a lively tune.

Toot passed Jenna a glass of foaming pop as she sat down on a handy rock.

"Hey, gerroff," shouted a voice. "Rocks have feelings too, you know."

Jenna leapt up. "Sorry," she gasped. "I forgot that everything in The Wardrobe can speak."

Jenna had a wonderful time. She made friends with everyone, including the rock, who even let her sit on him after a while.

Later in the evening, everyone gathered around to sing a song about how Jenna's gran had saved them from being burnt in the Tikuti Tribe's fire.

"She's wonderful," said Toot, after they'd finished singing. "She often pops in and she's even promised to find a safe place for The Wardrobe. A place where somebody will always look after us."

"Let's hear it for Jenna and her gran," shouted Toot. "Hip! Hip! Hooray! Hip! Hip! Hooray!"

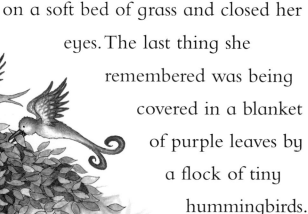

"Oooo! I feel a little sleepy," yawned Jenna, a little while later, after she had drunk her third nettle pop and eaten her fourth honey sandwich.

"I think I'll just lie down for a little while." She lay down on a soft bed of grass and closed her eyes. The last thing she remembered was being covered in a blanket of purple leaves by a flock of tiny hummingbirds.

When she awoke, she was no longer in The Wardrobe. She was in her own bed.

"I had the most fantastic dream," she told her mum and dad at breakfast.

"Well it looks like you've been climbing through a hedge," laughed Dad, pulling something out of her hair and handing it to her.

Jenna looked down to see what Dad had pulled out of her hair. It was a purple leaf. Jenna tingled with excitement. Her adventure in The Wardrobe must have been real, after all.

"Oh, yes," said Mum. "Gran called last night and said to tell you that you can keep the wardrobe. Can't see what you'd want with it though."

"Oh, well, things aren't always what they seem," smiled Jenna. "I will keep it safe forever."

Jenna just couldn't wait to pay her friends in The Wardrobe another visit! And she couldn't wait to tell Gran all about her adventure!

The Elves
and the Shoemaker

There was once a shoemaker who lived with his wife. The shoemaker worked very hard but he never made much money. In time, he became poorer and poorer. Then, one day, all he had left was one piece of leather. Just enough leather to make one pair of shoes. So, that night before going to bed, the shoemaker cut out the leather and left it on his workbench, ready to sew in the morning.

That night the shoemaker had a restless night's sleep as he worried about what they would do once the leather had gone. But, when the shoemaker went to the bench in the morning, he couldn't believe his eyes. In place of the cut-out bits of leather, there stood the finest pair of shoes he'd ever seen. Every stitch on them was so small and neat that they could hardly be seen.

"I've never seen such shoes," the shoemaker told his wife.

They couldn't think who could have sewn them, but they proudly displayed them in the window anyway.

Later that morning, a grand lady came into the shop and tried them on. "I've never worn anything so comfortable," she declared. The lady liked the shoes so much that she paid the shoemaker twice his normal price for them.

The shoemaker was delighted. Now he had money to buy food and enough leather to make two pairs of shoes.

That evening, he carefully cut out the two pairs of shoes. Then he left them on his workbench, ready to stitch in the morning.

The following morning, the shoemaker was delighted to see two pairs of shoes in place of the leather. Once again, they were beautifully stitched.

Later that day, a noble lord came into the shop to buy shoes. The shoemaker showed him the two pairs and he was so impressed that he tried both on. They fitted perfectly, so he bought both pairs for a lot of money.

Now the shoemaker had enough money to buy leather for four pairs of shoes.

That evening, before going to bed, he carefully cut out the four pairs of shoes and left them on the bench. Once again, he fully intended to stitch them in the morning.

However, when he awoke the following morning, he found four perfect pairs of shoes sitting on his workbench. Once again, he sold the shoes for a great deal of money.

From then on, each night the shoemaker cut out shoes ready to stitch in the morning and, each morning, he found in their place shoes so perfectly made that he couldn't see a bad stitch on them.

Day after day, rich customers came to the shoemaker's shop to buy the perfectly-made shoes. So, in time, the shoemaker and his wife became quite rich. But they never took their good fortune for granted.

One evening, just before Christmas, the shoemaker said to his wife, "Why don't we stay up this evening to see who it is who stitches our shoes?"

The shoemaker's wife quickly agreed. That night they hid behind some clothes hanging in the corner of the room and waited.

For a long time nothing happened, then at midnight two tiny, little men danced into the room. The two little men, whom the shoemaker recognised as elves, had bare feet and were dressed in rags.

The two elves did not see the shoemaker and his wife, but climbed up onto the bench, sat down and began stitching. They worked so fast that the shoemaker could barely believe his eyes.

They did not stop until all the work was done. Then they danced off into the night.

The following morning, the shoemaker and his wife agreed that they should repay the elves in some way. After all, they had made them rich.

So, that very day, they went out and bought the finest material and the softest leather they could find. That evening, they set to work making new clothes for the elves.

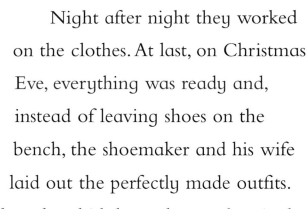

Night after night they worked on the clothes. At last, on Christmas Eve, everything was ready and, instead of leaving shoes on the bench, the shoemaker and his wife laid out the perfectly made outfits. Then they hid themselves and waited.

At midnight, the elves danced into the room and climbed up onto the bench. They were surprised to see tiny matching outfits instead of shoes for stitching. Delighted, they dressed themselves in their new clothes. Then, laughing and singing, they danced out into the night.

After that, the shoemaker and his wife never saw the elves again. But they did not mind. They had repaid the favour and from then on luck was always with them. In time they became very rich and lived a long and happy life together.

The Birthday Surprise

The Queen of the Fairies' birthday was on Midsummer's day and the fairies and elves of the forest were busy preparing for the party that evening.

Everyone had a job to do. The older ones were making fairy cakes, iced rose petals and dewdrop candies for the feast, while the youngsters were flitting around in search of acorn cups for the nectar juice. The crickets were practising their top ten hits in time for the disco and Strawberry, the Queen's head elf-in-waiting, had spent the whole morning laying clues for a fairy treasure hunt.

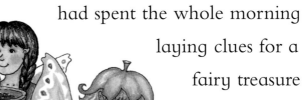

Daffodil, Rose and Holly were trying to hang a huge banner from the branches of the oak tree, but not with very much success.

"Left a bit, right a bit, up a bit…" called Holly, from the forest floor. "No, down a bit, left a bit…"

"For goodness sake, make your mind up!" complained Daffodil, hovering high up in the branches of the oak tree. "Our wings are going to drop off soon!"

"That will have to do!" said Rose, fluttering down to the ground. "We've got heaps of other jobs to do before the party starts. I've still got a hundred honey-coated, dreamy-cream puffs to make…"

"Don't forget we've got to decorate the Queen's throne with blossom," added Holly. "We haven't even picked the flowers yet."

They all looked at each other in dismay. "Oops! I'd forgotten about that," gulped Rose.

23

"We'd better get going right away. I know a glade where there are some beautiful pink roses. We can use those…"

"Not pink again," moaned Holly. "It's always pink, pink, pink with you! Why can't we have green leaves instead?"

"GREEN!" exclaimed Daffodil. "We don't want green leaves, or pink flowers for that matter. What we need are some sunny yellow flowers for a change."

"That's typical of you two!" cried Rose, beginning to lose her temper. "You never listen to what I want to do."

I'm ashamed to say that Daffodil, Rose and Holly were soon squabbling like kindergarten fairies.

"GREEN!" cried Holly.

"YELLOW!" yelled Daffodil.

"PINK!" shouted Rose, at the top of her voice.

"What on earth is going on?" interrupted a surprised voice. It was Strawberry. He had come to see what all the fuss was about. He listened quietly as the three fairies explained what had started the argument. When they had finished, he shook his head slowly. "There's no need for all this shouting!" he said wisely. "There's only one fair way to settle a question like this. We must hold a pow-wow in the fairy ring."

As Strawberry waved his wand in a circle, tiny red and white spotted mushrooms pushed up through the warm earth to make a perfect ring around them. Then he took a shell from his pocket and blew into it like a horn. The sound of the shell called all the other fairies to the glade and before long the air was filled with the sound of chattering voices.

Strawberry raised
his hands for silence. "I've
called a pow-wow so that we
can decide what colour flowers to use
to decorate the Queen's throne," he
announced. "If you want to suggest a
colour, you must step into the ring and tell
everyone why you have chosen it. At the end of
the pow-wow, I will choose the winner."

Holly cleared her throat, then stepped forward bravely
into the fairy ring. "Everyone knows that our Queen
loves the green, green forest," she said, "and that's
why I think we should choose the colour green."

It was Daffodil's turn next. "The Queen
loves golden yellow sunshine," she told
the crowd. "That's why I think we
should choose yellow."

"Pink is the colour
of her favourite blossom," whispered
Rose, who felt rather shy in front of everyone.

"Red is the colour of summer strawberries," suggested
another little fairy, "and the Queen loves strawberries.
Maybe we should decorate the throne red!"

"The Queen may love strawberries in summer,"
announced one fairy confidently, "but juicy purple plums are
her favourite in autumn. I think we should choose purple."

"Why don't we choose orange, like the sunset," said
someone else. "Her Majesty always says that's the most
beautiful time of day."

"You're all wrong!" cried one very excited
fairy. "Blue is the colour of the sky and
the river. You know how the Queen
loves to lie on the river bank and
gaze at the sky."

Finally, when everyone who wanted to speak had said his or her piece, the glade fell silent. Everyone looked at Strawberry, expectantly. Which colour would he choose?

But Strawberry didn't give his answer. He just smiled mysteriously. "Rose, Daffodil and Holly," he said, his eyes sparkling with fun. "Come with me. We have work to do. The Queen's throne needs decorating!"

Later that evening, it was amid much excitement that the fairies made their way through the forest to the birthday party. What delicious things would there be to eat? Who would dance with them at the party? Most importantly, what colour would the flowers around the Queen's throne be?

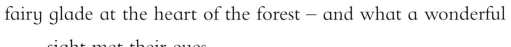

Glow-worms lit the way like candles, as the cricket music beckoned the fairies on through the trees. Finally, they emerged into the fairy glade at the heart of the forest – and what a wonderful sight met their eyes.

HAPPY BIRTHDAY

There on the throne sat the Queen. Arching around
her like a rainbow, were flowers of every colour.

"Welcome, everyone!" she smiled graciously.
"Thank you for my party and thank you most of
all for the beautiful flower decorations.
Strawberry has told me why each colour flower
was chosen! What a perfect gift for my birthday!"

The fairies of the forest glowed
with pride, but no one was
more proud than Rose,
Daffodil and Holly.

Cinderella

Long ago, in a distant land, lived a man with his beautiful daughter. They were both very happy, until one day the man took a new wife. The new wife was not a kind woman and, to make matters worse, she had two bad-tempered daughters. The two daughters were so mean and so ugly that they were jealous of the man's beautiful daughter. Indeed, they were so jealous that they took away all her fine clothes and forced her to work as their maid.

The poor girl worked from dawn to dusk. She cooked all the meals, cleaned all the rooms and looked after all the fires. When she wasn't working around the house, the ugly sisters insisted that she dress them and brush their hair.

At night, while the ugly sisters snored away in their fine beds, their beautiful stepsister huddled among the cinders beside the fire. This was the reason why she always looked so dusty and sooty and why everyone called her Cinderella.

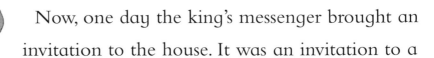

Now, one day the king's messenger brought an invitation to the house. It was an invitation to a ball that the king was giving for his son, the prince. All the young girls in the land were invited, so that the prince could choose a bride.

The ugly sisters were delighted and immediately started discussing what they were going to wear.

"Can I come, too?" asked Cinderella. "I've never been to a ball."

"Of course you can't, silly," laughed Cinderella's stepmother, pointing to the rags she wore. "What would you wear? Besides, no prince would bother looking at a silly, sooty face like yours. But don't worry, you can help my girls get dressed for the ball."

On the evening of the ball, the ugly sisters took ages getting ready. Poor old Cinderella's head whirled as they barked orders at her.

"Tighter, tighter!" cried one, as Cinderella struggled to fasten a corset around her huge waist.

"Ouch! That hurt!" snapped the other, as Cinderella tried to tease the knots from her tangled hair.

When at last they left for the ball, Cinderella fell to the floor and wept. "If only I could go to the ball," she sobbed.

"But, you shall," said a kind voice. Cinderella wiped the tears from her eyes and looked up to see her fairy godmother standing before her.

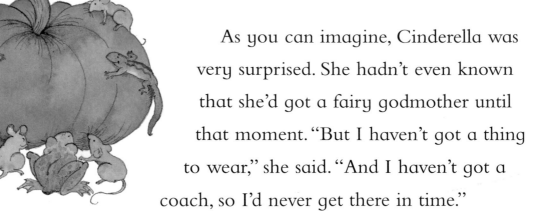

As you can imagine, Cinderella was very surprised. She hadn't even known that she'd got a fairy godmother until that moment. "But I haven't got a thing to wear," she said. "And I haven't got a coach, so I'd never get there in time."

"Just fetch these things," said the fairy godmother, pulling out a list from up her sleeve, "and I'll get you there before you know it."

Cinderella looked at the list and frowned. But, being a good girl, she quickly did as she was asked. Five minutes later, she returned with the things on the list: a pumpkin, six white mice, a frog and two lizards.

Her fairy godmother drew out her magic wand and touched the pumpkin. Immediately it turned into a golden coach.

Then she touched the mice with her wand and they turned into six white horses. Next, she touched the frog, which turned into a smart coachman. Finally, she touched the two lizards, who turned into two well-dressed footmen.

"Now for you," said the fairy godmother, pointing her wand at Cinderella. Instantly, Cinderella's rags were transformed into a fine velvet ball gown and the clogs she normally wore on her feet were turned into delicate, glass slippers.

"Now, go to your ball and enjoy yourself," said the fairy godmother. "But remember this. You must leave the ball before midnight, for on the stroke of twelve the magic will run out and all will be as it was before."

35

The footmen helped Cinderella into the coach, the coachman took up the reins and they were on their way.

When Cinderella arrived at the ball, everyone gasped at her beauty. "May I have this dance?" asked the prince.

Naturally, Cinderella agreed.

For the rest of the evening, the prince would dance with no other. Cinderella's ugly sisters didn't recognise her, dressed as she was in such fine clothes. But they were still furious. "I can't think what the prince can see in her, she's nothing but a skinny beanpole," sneered one. "Barely a jewel in sight," sneered the other. It was the best evening of Cinderella's life.

She enjoyed herself so much that she almost forgot about her fairy godmother's warning. Then, just before twelve, she remembered.

"I must leave," she told the prince. Before he could stop her, she had fled into the night. But, as she raced out of the palace, she slipped on the steps and lost one of her glass slippers. She dared not stop. She didn't even notice that the prince picked up the slipper.

Then, as the clock struck twelve, Cinderella's ball gown vanished and she found herself in her rags once more. When she got to where she had left the coach, she found the pumpkin in its place.

Poor Cinderella had to run all the way home. She only just made it before her stepmother and stepsisters returned.

The following day, the prince announced that he would travel the kingdom in search of the owner of the dainty slipper. "Every girl in the kingdom will try it for size," he declared, "for whoever it fits is the one I love and the one I will make my bride."

Of course, every girl in the kingdom was eager to marry the prince. Girls of all shapes and sizes tried to squeeze their foot into the tiny slipper but, it was too small.

At last, the prince arrived at Cinderella's house. Cinderella's stepmother was determined that one of her daughters would become the prince's bride.

"Push harder," she hissed, trying to wedge the glass slipper on one of her daughter's feet.

"Can't you do anything right?" she complained, when her other daughter couldn't even get the slipper over her knobbly toes.

"Don't you have another daughter?" asked the prince, when Cinderella's stepmother finally admitted defeat.

"There is only Cinderella," she said, "and she's little more than a maid."

But the prince insisted that Cinderella try on the slipper and, of course, it fitted her perfectly. The prince peered at the shabby figure before him and smiled. Even through the dirt and grime, he could recognise the beautiful maiden he had danced with.

"My one true love," he cried, before lifting her onto his horse and riding away.

Prince Grizzly-Beard

Once upon a time, there was a king who had a beautiful daughter. The king wanted his daughter to marry a prince and so he invited all the princes from far and wide to try to win her hand.

But the princess made fun of all the princes who visited the castle. One she thought too red faced and called him 'Pinkychops'. Another she thought too thin and called him 'Bandylegs'. One, whose beard she disliked, she called, 'Prince Grizzly-Beard'.

"Look at this silly mop," she laughed, tugging the prince's beard. The princess's father was furious. "I've had enough," he declared. "I'm going to marry you off to the very first man who comes to the castle door."

The princess thought her father's threat was just a joke and continued to laugh about 'Prince Grizzly-Beard' long after all the princes had left. She was still laughing when the first man to call at the castle door turned out to be a ragged beggar.

"What a good joke!" she laughed, when her father told her that she had to marry the beggar. But she stopped laughing when a parson was summoned to conduct the marriage service. She realised that the king wasn't joking at all.

Before she knew it, the princess was married. "But where shall we live?" she wailed, glaring at the beggar who was now her husband.

"Don't worry," he smiled. "I've got a beautiful hut on the other side of the wood."

"A hut!" wailed the princess. "I can't live in a hut!"

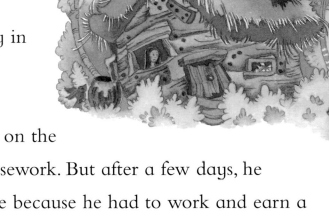

But, because her father said she had no choice, the beautiful princess found herself living in a humble hut. To make matters worse, it lay in the kingdom that belonged to Prince Grizzly-Beard's father.

At first, the beggar took pity on the princess and helped with the housework. But after a few days, he declared that she must do it alone because he had to work and earn a living. After a few more days, the beggar told her that she had to earn her keep and sent her to market with china pots to sell.

The princess had never been so ashamed in her life. She was terrified that someone she knew might see her and hid herself at the back of the market. But, even so, the first day's trade went remarkably well, for, on seeing such a beautiful maid selling pots, lots of people came to buy them.

On the second day, the princess set out her stall in a better position, where more people passed by. But disaster struck when a soldier stumbled over her pots and smashed the lot.

When she told her husband what
had happened, he was very cross. "I can
see that you're not fit for selling pots.
Luckily, I've arranged for you to work as
a kitchen maid in the king's castle."

So the princess became a kitchen maid and
had to scrub floors and clean lots of very dirty pans.

The princess hadn't been working at the castle very
long when the king announced that his son, the
prince, was to be married. The castle was
decorated in the richest jewels and the finest
food was cooked. As the princess helped prepare
for the wedding, she wept.

"To think that I would still
have been a princess if only I
had agreed to marry Prince
Grizzly-Beard," she sobbed.

As she was about to
leave the castle gate on
the day before the
wedding, a handsome
bearded figure came
towards her and took
her hand.

He led her into the ballroom. "May I have this dance?" he asked. The poor princess trembled with shame, for she had recognised the handsome figure as Prince Grizzly-Beard. Surely, he had come to tease her?

However, he kept hold of her hand and whisked her around the dance floor, much to the amusement of his friends who thought it really funny that the prince should make such fun of a lowly kitchen maid.

The princess was so ashamed that she wished she could disappear into the floor. But then, Prince Grizzly-Beard spoke in a kind voice:

"Fear not," he smiled. "I'm not just dancing with you for fun. Don't you recognise me? I am your husband – the beggar. I disguised myself as a beggar and called at your father's door so that you would have to marry me. I am also the soldier who broke all your pots in the marketplace."

"But why have you done all this to me?" cried the princess.

"Because I love you and wanted to cure you of your silly ways. I also wanted to show you how much it hurts to be laughed at by others. But now it is over, we can have another wedding feast here, in my father's castle."

The princess was furious but, before very long, she saw that Prince Grizzly-Beard had only been kind so that she would be cured of being too proud and mean to other people.

From that day on, Prince Grizzly-Beard and his princess lived happily ever after. In time they became king and queen – the kindest king and queen that the kingdom had ever known.

The Swineherd

Once upon a time, there was a poor prince. He was very kind and handsome. Many fine ladies would have been happy to marry him. However the prince only wished to marry the Emperor's beautiful daughter. She, on the other hand, had other ideas.

"You're far too poor," she said. "You might own a palace and have enough money for an ordinary girl, but you just don't have any gold to keep me in the jewels and gifts I deserve." With that she pushed him out of her father's palace and told him not to come calling on her again.

The prince might not have been as rich as your average prince, but he had two things far better than gold.

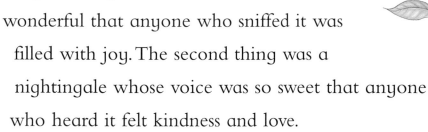

Firstly, he had a rose bush that grew a single rose every five years; its perfume smelled so wonderful that anyone who sniffed it was filled with joy. The second thing was a nightingale whose voice was so sweet that anyone who heard it felt kindness and love.

The prince decided to give these two things to the Emperor's daughter. He was sure that as soon as she saw them, she would want to become his bride. He packed them in two wooden caskets and delivered them himself.

The Emperor's daughter opened the first casket. When she took out the rose, she threw it down in disgust.

"It's just a smelly old rose," she cried. Its perfume didn't fill her with joy.

She opened the second casket and out flew the nightingale. As it began to sing, the Emperor and his courtiers clapped their hands with glee. The Emperor's daughter just frowned.

"Why would I want a silly old bird?" she asked, for the nightingale's song didn't fill her with kindness and love.

She had the prince thrown from her father's palace. "As if I'd marry anyone who gave me such silly gifts," she shouted, throwing the wooden caskets out of the window.

Although the prince was upset, he still wanted to marry the Emperor's daughter.

The next day, he dressed as a beggar and called at the palace looking for work.

"I have just the job for you," said the Emperor, looking at the prince's ragged clothes. "I need someone to look after my pigs."

So the beggar prince became the royal swineherd. Each morning he tended the pigs, and each afternoon he sat outside his hut making things.

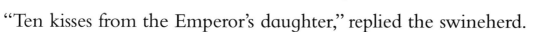

One afternoon, he made a silver cooking pot, covered in golden bells. When the pot boiled, the silver bells tinkled a little tune.

When the Emperor's daughter saw the silver pot and heard the lovely tune it tinkled, she wanted it for herself. She sent her servant to ask the swineherd what he wanted for the pot.

"Ten kisses from the Emperor's daughter," replied the swineherd.

The Emperor's daughter was furious. "How dare he!" she shouted. But when the bells began to tinkle once more, she marched to where the swineherd sat.

"Very well. You shall have your kisses," she said. "But I don't want to be seen by anyone."

She made a group of servants gather round her and the swineherd got his ten kisses. He should have been happy, but he couldn't help thinking that the Emperor's daughter was spoilt.

The next day, the swineherd made a beautiful golden rattle.

When it was swung in the air it played
wonderful tunes.

"I must have it," said the Emperor's
daughter. Once again, she sent her servant to find out what
the swineherd wanted for it.

"One hundred kisses from the Emperor's daughter," he replied.

After a little protest, the Emperor's daughter agreed. Once again,
she made her servants gather round while she kissed the swineherd.
As the servants counted the kisses, the swineherd couldn't help thinking
that perhaps the Emperor's daughter was too spoilt and greedy to
make a good wife.

But before he had time to say anything, the Emperor, who

happened to be walking by, spotted the gaggle of
servants gathered in a circle around
the swineherd's hut.

"What's going on here?" he
demanded. As you can imagine,
he was furious when he
discovered that his daughter was
being kissed by the swineherd.

"How dare you," he
shouted and straight away had his
daughter and the swineherd
thrown out of the palace.

The Emperor's
daughter stamped
her foot and cried.

"If only I'd married the
handsome prince who gave
me the rose and the
nightingale," she wailed.

The swineherd
disappeared for a
moment, then reappeared dressed as a prince.

The prince looked sadly at the Emperor's daughter.
"I'm sorry," he said, "but I don't think I can marry you. You
are just too silly. After all, you didn't want my lovely rose and
nightingale, but were willing to kiss a swineherd for the sake of a
few glittering trinkets."

Then, with a sad farewell, he went back to his
own little kingdom.

As for the Emperor's
daughter? Well, her father
eventually let her back into
the palace, but only
after she'd promised
never to be quite
so silly again!

The Little Dragon Learns to Fly

Long, long ago, a fierce dragon lived in a mountain cave above a village called Dragonia. Nobody had actually seen the dragon, but many people had seen the hot flames of dragon's breath that poured from the cave when anybody went too close.

One day, a little boy called Jake was picking wild flowers near the cave when he stubbed his toe on what looked like a rock.

"Ouch!" said the rock, which jumped up and hid behind a bigger rock. It gave Jake quite a shock.

It wasn't a rock at all.

"I was having a n…n…n…nap," complained a frightened voice.

"Who are you?" asked Jake.

"I'm the d…d…d…dragon and if you d…d…d…don't go away I shall b…b…b…b…breathe fire all over you," stuttered the voice. After a pause it added, "Are you big?"

"I'm bigger than my brother," said Jake. "I'm seven."

A green head, with knobbles, pointed ears and nostrils on stalks, peered round the rock.

"That's funny," said the dragon. "I'm seven as well."

He came out from behind the rock. He was a surprisingly small dragon. In fact, he was no taller than Jake, with stumpy wings on his back no bigger than Jake's hands.

"Can you fly?" asked Jake.

"I've never tried," said the dragon.

"Never?" gasped Jake.

"No, never." The very idea of flying made him tremble. "Now, please go away and don't tell anyone I'm only a small dragon, or people will start poking about in my cave and frighten me." He disappeared out of sight.

By the time Jake reached the village he was bursting to tell someone about the little dragon. But when he remembered how scared he had been he decided not to. That would have been that, if the villagers hadn't been so poor that they held a meeting to decide how to get rich.

"I know," suggested the butcher, "let's get a knight to slay the dragon and charge money for people to watch."

That was in the days when people did that sort of thing, so the villagers all agreed it was a brilliant idea. They invited the local knight to fight the dragon.

You should have seen the crowd that turned up. They all cheered like mad when the knight set off up the mountain. Jake didn't see him go. He was already scurrying up the mountain to warn the dragon. Because he was in such a hurry, he didn't look where he was going and slipped.

"Ahhhh!" he cried, as he hurtled helter-skelter down the side of the mountain! He landed with a bump on a narrow ledge.

"Help! Help!" he called. But nobody heard, except the dragon who was soon peering down at him.

"Help me," begged Jake.

"What?" asked the dragon, who was quaking with fear. "How can I possibly help?"

"Couldn't you flap your wings and fly to my rescue?" asked Jake.

"Don't be silly! I've never flown in my life," replied the dragon.

"But," pleaded Jake, "I was climbing up the mountain to warn you that a knight is coming to kill you."

"Ooooooh," said the dragon. "I'm off!"

Poor Jake. He was so frightened that he couldn't help crying. The dragon, who hadn't gone very far, knew a great deal about crying. It was very lonely being a dragon, and living on your own, so he cried a lot.

"Please don't cry," he said, peering down at Jake again.

"But I might die."

"Oh dear, couldn't you climb back up?"

"No!" sobbed Jake.

"I don't believe you've tried!" said the dragon, crossly. He stamped his foot so hard that the ground beneath him began to crumble and he began to fall.

"WHOOOOAH!" he cried, as he hurtled down the side of the mountain.

"Ooooooh!" he yelled, whizzing past the narrow ledge where Jake sat.

"Flap your wings and fly!" yelled Jake.

"Oooooooh," sobbed the dragon.

"Fly!" begged Jake.

Goodness knows what made the dragon twitch his wings. But something did. The next moment, he was flying!

"Look, look, I can fly!" he gasped, scooping Jake from the ledge and flap-flapping to the top of the mountain.

"How about that?" he laughed, dropping Jake, not very gently, at the mouth of the dragon's cave.

"Ah, there you are!" panted a voice. It was the knight. He was out of breath from hurrying up the mountain in his heavy suit of armour.

"Please, don't kill the dragon," begged Jake.

"Y…yes, please don't kill me," quaked the dragon.

"I wouldn't dream of it," exclaimed the knight. "Why, I saw this brave dragon throw himself off the mountain just so he could fly to your rescue. It was one of the bravest things I've ever seen."

Which is what the knight told the villagers when he brought Jake down the mountain.

The villagers were so pleased that they threw a special feast in honour of the little dragon. There was dancing and singing, sandwiches, cakes and lots and lots to drink. Everyone had a splendid time, including the little dragon, who Jake managed to persuade to join them.

The little dragon made so many new friends that he couldn't remember all their names. He'd never been so happy. Indeed, he was so happy that he decided to share his treasure with all the villagers, for, as I'm sure you know, all dragons guard over a hoard of treasure.

As a result, the villagers were no longer poor, the dragon was no longer lonely and everybody lived happily ever after!

Beauty and the Beast

Once upon a time, there was a rich merchant who lived in a grand house with his three beautiful daughters. The girls were given everything they wanted and were waited on by an army of servants.

The two eldest sisters were very vain and very spoiled but the youngest, who was also the prettiest, was kind and sweet. Indeed, she was so pretty and kind that everyone called her 'Beauty'.

All three girls led a fine life and couldn't have been happier. Then, one day, disaster struck. Their father lost his fortune and so they had to move to a tiny cottage in the wood. The two eldest girls were not at all happy and spent every day grumbling and squabbling. But Beauty couldn't have been happier. She loved the little cottage and enjoyed cleaning it and tending its little garden.

So they settled into their new life, until one day their father
was called away on business. It was a trip that
promised to help give them back their fortune, so
you can imagine how everyone was excited. Before
he left, the merchant asked each of his
daughters what present she would
like him to bring back. The two
elder girls reeled off an endless list.

"Pearl necklace… diamond brooch… velvet
gown… silk scarves… gold ring…" said one.

"Emerald bracelet… sapphire earrings… silk gown…
silver comb… gold slippers…" said the other.

However, when the merchant asked
Beauty what she would like, she thought
for a moment, then said, "What I
would wish for most of all is a single
red rose. We have none in our
garden and I do love them so."

This simple request brought
a tear to the merchant's
eye that stayed with
him throughout his
long journey.

The trip proved a success and the merchant travelled home a much richer man. He had bought the dresses and jewels the elder daughters had asked for and was searching for a red rose for Beauty when he became quite lost.

As night began to fall, the weary traveller looked around for shelter and was surprised to come across a grand palace hidden deep in the wood. On the palace gates was a bold sign, which read:

WELCOME
ALL
TRAVELLERS

As the merchant approached the gates, they swung open as if inviting him in. The merchant looked around, but no one was there. He shrugged his shoulders in surprise, then hurried to put his horse in the well-kept, but empty, stable. After he had fed and watered the horse, he knocked on the palace door. No one answered but the palace door swung open.

The merchant wandered through the palace. All the rooms were richly furnished and fires burned in all the grates, but no one was there. In one of the rooms, a tempting meal was laid out on a table. The merchant waited to see if anyone would come, but eventually hunger got the better of him and he sat down to dine alone.

When he had finished eating, the merchant looked around for a place to sleep. In one of the bedrooms, the bed was made and, remembering the sign on the gate, the merchant spent the night there.

The following morning, he awoke to find his clothes washed and neatly folded. When he went downstairs, a fine breakfast was waiting.

After breakfast, the merchant decided to take a walk in the garden before leaving. It was a beautiful morning and the flowers in the garden were beyond compare. As he walked beneath a climbing rose, the merchant remembered Beauty's request and reached up to pluck a single red rose.

As soon as he held the rose in his hand, he heard a terrible roar. Terrified, he turned to find an ugly beast racing towards him.

"How dare you steal my prize rose," snarled the Beast. "Is that how you repay me for letting you stay in my home?"

"But, I was just picking the rose for my youngest daughter," began the merchant.

"I don't care," said the Beast. "You will pay heavily for your crime. You will become my prisoner and never leave this place."

Thinking of his poor daughters, who would surely starve without him, the merchant begged to be let go.

Eventually, the Beast agreed on the condition that one of the merchant's daughters came to live in the palace.

The merchant returned home with a heavy heart. Upon hearing his story, Beauty insisted that she went to live with the Beast. Reluctantly, and after much argument, the merchant finally agreed.

When the merchant took Beauty to the palace, it was just as empty as on his first visit. But after they had eaten a meal, the Beast appeared. Beauty had never seen anything so ugly, but she tried to hide her fear.

"So you have come in your father's place," said the Beast, as gently as he could. "You must love him very much."

"Yes," nodded Beauty, trying not to shrink away.

"You are a kind girl," said the Beast. "I will treat you well."

Seeing that the Beast was so gentle with Beauty, the merchant felt less worried as he returned home.

So Beauty's new life began. She spent each day alone in the palace, then in the evening was joined by the Beast. In time, Beauty grew quite fond of the Beast and always looked forward to his company.

At the end of each evening, just before leaving, the Beast would say, "Will you marry me, Beauty?"

Beauty would always reply, politely, "No thank you, Beast."

Then the Beast would give a heavy sigh and leave. But the following evening he would ask her again. Again Beauty would reply, "No thank you, Beast."

It made Beauty sad to think that she made the Beast unhappy, but there was no way she could marry such an ugly creature.

Beauty hadn't been living in the palace for very long when she began to feel homesick. When the Beast, who was really quite kind and cared greatly for Beauty, realised what was wrong, he gave her an enchanted mirror.

Whenever Beauty looked into the mirror, she could see her family. In this way, she always knew what was happening in her father's house.

Beauty looked into the mirror each day and each day was pleased to see her family looking happy. They had moved back into their big house and her father's business was doing well. Her sisters, who were as vain as ever, both found husbands and left home. Beauty was pleased for them, but felt sad to think that she would never be a bride.

Then one day, Beauty was feeling particularly homesick. She looked into her mirror to cheer herself up but got a terrible shock. For there was her father ill in bed, with both of her sisters weeping at his side.

When the Beast came that evening, he saw that something was wrong and asked Beauty what was troubling her. Beauty quickly explained and begged the Beast to let her visit her father.

65

After much thought, the Beast reluctantly agreed to let her go, but he made her promise she wouldn't stay away for long.

The following morning when Beauty awoke, she found herself not in the Beast's palace but in her father's house. As soon as her father saw her, his heart lifted and from that day on he began to get better.

Some weeks had passed and her father had been well for some time, when Beauty remembered her promise to the Beast. She looked into her magic mirror and was alarmed to see the Beast alone and dying. Immediately, she arranged for her father to take her back to the Beast's palace.

On arriving, she found the Beast lying beneath his beloved climbing rose. "Please don't die," cried Beauty. "I couldn't live without you."

"I thought you'd forgotten all about me and would never come back," said the Beast. "Without you, I had nothing to live for."

"Forgive me," sobbed Beauty. "When I saw you were ill, I realised that I love you. I will marry you, if you'll still have me."

As soon as she whispered those words, the Beast changed into a handsome prince!

The prince quickly explained that an evil witch had cast a spell, turning him into a Beast – a spell that could only be broken when somebody loved him and promised to marry him.

Beauty was delighted with her handsome prince and couldn't wait to tell her father of her good fortune. Not long after, Beauty and the prince were married and in her hands, Beauty carried a bunch of roses from the Beast's rose bush.

Shimmer and the River

"How many times have I asked you not to wander off?" said Shimmer the Mermaid's mum, as they swam home from a visit to the surface. "You know you're not allowed to go near the river on the beach."

"Why not?" asked Shimmer. "What's wrong with swimming near the river?"

But Shimmer's mother was in too much of a hurry to answer questions. "Not now, Shimmer," she said, impatiently. "Just come along. I'm far too busy to float around arguing with you."

Just then, Swoop the Seagull landed on a large rock nearby.

"YOO-HOO! Swoop, dear!" called Shimmer's mum, flashing through the water with a huge swish of her tail. "I just wanted to have a quick word with you. Have you got a moment?"

"I thought we were in a hurry!" Shimmer muttered, sitting on a ledge. "We'll be here forever now!"

Suddenly, the bored little mermaid caught sight of a shoal of angel fish, darting through the water. "How lovely!" she cried, forgetting all about not wandering off. With a flick of her tail, she swam off to play chase with the multi-coloured fish. In and out of the rocks they darted, chasing through underwater archways as they went.

Just when Shimmer had nearly caught them up, the shoal turned in a flash and disappeared into a cave.

"You can't escape!" laughed Shimmer, following them. "I know you're in here!" But there was no sign of the glittering shoal. Shimmer swam deeper and deeper down the cave's tunnels, searching for her friends. "Stop hiding!" she called, her voice echoing around.

Shimmer began to feel a little worried. It was dark in the tunnel and there was no sign of anyone at all.

"I think it's time I turned back," she said to herself, remembering her mother's warnings. "But which way do I go?" Shimmer tried first one tunnel, then another, but none of them seemed to lead in the direction of home. She was lost!

"I'll just have to choose one tunnel and go for it!" she decided, swimming off down one that seemed a little brighter than the rest. "This one has to come out somewhere!"

Shimmer had been swimming for what seemed like ages, when she began to notice something strange. As the light at the end of the tunnel got brighter, the water began to get warmer – and it tasted rather funny, too. There was no salt in it!

Finally, she popped out at the end of the tunnel in a large still pool. Shimmer rubbed her eyes in amazement. This pool was like no other she had ever seen. There was no yellow sand or seaweed in sight. Instead, the edge of the silver pool was soft velvety green, with strange plants growing all around it.

"I must have come out in the river!" she gasped, gazing about her. "How beautiful it all is. I wonder why we're not allowed to come here!"

Just then, Shimmer heard a loud cough and turned round to see a large, green frog sitting on a nearby rock. "You're very unusual for a fish!" it croaked.

"But I'm not a fish!" exclaimed Shimmer in surprise. "I'm a mermaid. I live in the ocean!"

"In the ocean!" exclaimed the frog, grinning from ear to ear. "How wonderful to meet someone from the OCEAN!" Then he gave a very loud croak. Slowly, all sorts of woodland creatures began to peep out from behind the bushes to say hello.

"They ran and hid when they first saw you," chuckled the frog. "We've never seen a mermaid before! Please will you tell us all about life in the ocean?" So, Shimmer began to describe her home to the animals.

She told them about the games of chase she played with the fish, about the friendly dolphins, the grumpy crabs and lobsters, about the beautiful coral reef and the sea anemones that lived on it.

She was so busy talking to her new friends that she didn't notice a shadow swooping over the pond. Suddenly, there was a loud splash as Swoop the Seagull landed in the water beside her.

"Thank goodness I've found you!" squawked the gull. "We must leave immediately! Hurry! I will show you the shortcut back to the ocean."

"It's not fair! " said Shimmer, crossly. "I don't want to go home yet. I bet Mum sent you to fetch me!"

Swoop looked very serious. "She did," he said. "And it's a very good job she did. Mermaids become ill if they stay in water without salt for too long. If you don't believe me, look at your scales!"

Sure enough, Shimmer's once-glittering scales were colourless and dull.

"I'm sorry, Swoop!" apologised Shimmer, looking shame-faced. "I didn't mean to cause so much trouble. From now on I'll try and listen to what Mum says. It's just that I've made lots of new friends here and now I won't be able to keep in touch with them!"

Swoop thought carefully for a moment. "Don't worry!" he squawked. "I can deliver messages for you. I often pass this way."

Shimmer and the woodland animals were delighted at the suggestion. "We can send each other news by Seagull Post!" laughed Shimmer, waving goodbye to her new friends. Then, with a flick of her tail, she disappeared beneath the water and headed back to the salty ocean, where mermaids belong.

The Twelve Dancing Princesses

Once upon a time, there was a king who had twelve beautiful daughters. During the day, the girls were model princesses. But at night, the king didn't know what they got up to. It was very puzzling, because although he carefully locked the door to their room, by morning all their shoes were worn out as if they had been out dancing all night long.

Buying new shoes for his twelve princess daughters was costing the king a lot of money and he was getting annoyed.

The king announced that whoever discovered where the twelve princesses danced at night could choose his favourite for his bride.

Before long, twelve noble princes took up the challenge. Each one sat guard, in a chair, beside a princess's bed. But before the clock struck twelve, the princes were all asleep. When they awoke in the morning, the princesses had clearly been dancing because their shoes were full of holes. So, the twelve princes left the kingdom empty-handed.

One day, a poor soldier was passing through the forest near the castle, when he met an old woman who lived there. "Where are you going?" she asked the soldier.

"I thought I'd go and find out where the princesses dance each night," he explained.

"I see," cackled the old woman. "Well, that shouldn't be too hard. But make sure you don't drink anything those princesses offer you." Then she gave him a cloak. "As soon as you put this on you will be invisible," she explained. "That way, you will be able to follow the princesses without them knowing it."

So the poor soldier went to the castle to try his luck. That night, as he prepared to sit guard, the eldest princess brought him a glass of water. Remembering the old woman's warning, the soldier threw the water away. Then he lay back and pretended to snore.

When the princesses heard his snores, they started to dress. After they'd pulled on the new shoes that the king had bought that very day, they checked that the soldier was still sleeping. Satisfied that the sleeping potion she had given him had worked, the eldest princess went to her bed and clapped her hands.

The soldier, who was peeping through half-closed eyes, was amazed to see the bed sink into the floor and a trap door swing open. He watched quietly as each of the princesses went through the trap door, one by one.

When the last princess had disappeared, the soldier leapt to his feet, threw the cloak around his shoulders and became invisible.

Thinking that there wasn't a moment to lose, he raced down the stairs so fast that he trod on the youngest princess's dress.

"Someone has hold of my gown," cried the princess. But the other princesses told her not to be so silly and hurried her along.

At the bottom of the stairs, the soldier followed the princesses through a door into beautiful woodland. The silver leaves on the trees sparkled so brilliantly that the soldier decided to break one off in order to take it home.

"What was that?" said the youngest princess. "I'm sure someone is following us."

The other princesses told her not to be silly and hurried her along.

At the edge of the wood, they came to a lake. At the side of the lake lay twelve boats, with twelve handsome princes waiting beside them. By the time a princess and a prince had got into each of the boats, they looked so overloaded that the soldier thought they would sink if he got in as well.

He eyed each of the princesses in turn. "Who is the lightest?" he wondered. Finally, he decided that the youngest princess was the lightest by far. But even as he got into the boat, it rocked and creaked.

Half way across the lake, the prince rowing the boat containing the youngest princess and the invisible soldier complained that it felt heavier than usual. "Have you put on weight?" he asked the princess.

"Don't be silly," said the youngest princess and she hurried him on his way.

On the other side of the lake was a golden castle. The soldier followed the twelve princes and twelve princesses into the castle and watched them dance the whole night through.

Then, just before dawn, still covered by his invisible coat, he followed the princesses home.

When they reached the stairs leading to their bedroom, the soldier overtook them, threw off his cloak and lay snoring in the chair before any of the princesses had climbed into the room through the trapdoor.

Seeing the soldier still fast asleep, the princesses thought their secret was safe.

The following morning, the soldier took the silver leaf he had broken from a branch to the king and explained what he had seen.

The king was very happy and asked which of the princesses he would choose for his bride.

The soldier chose the youngest, whom he thought prettier and smarter than any of her sisters. She was delighted, for she thought the soldier even handsomer than her prince.

Shortly after this, the soldier and the princess were married. Afterwards, there was a wonderful ball. The youngest princess danced with her new husband until midnight.

As for her eleven sisters? Well, they danced until dawn!

Snow White

Once, there were a king and queen who lived in a distant land. They were very happy, except for one thing – they had no children.

"Oh," said the queen, "how I wish I had a daughter with skin as white as snow, hair as black as a raven's wing and lips as red as cherries."

Within a year the queen's wish was granted and they had a beautiful baby girl, whom they called Snow White. Soon after her birth, the poor queen died and the king eventually remarried.

The new queen was very beautiful, but also very vain and very wicked. She could not bear to think that anyone was more beautiful than her. Every day she would stand in front of a magic mirror and say:

"Mirror, mirror, on the wall, Who is the fairest of them all?" And the mirror would reply: *"You are the fairest one of all."*

However, as the years passed, Snow White grew up to become more and more beautiful, until one day the magic mirror told the wicked queen: *"You were the fairest, shining bright, But now much fairer is Snow White."* The queen was furious. She sent for a servant. She told the servant to take Snow White into the forest and leave her there for the wild animals to eat.

So it was that Snow White found herself alone in the forest. At first she was scared, but soon the animals took pity on her and led her to a pretty little cottage. She knocked on the door and, when there was no answer, she walked right in. The inside of the cottage was as pretty as the outside. In the middle of the room stood a neat little table, set with seven places and surrounded by seven little chairs.

Feeling hungry and thirsty, Snow White took a little bread from each of the plates and a little milk from each of the cups. Then, feeling tired, she curled up on one of the seven beds and fell into a deep sleep.

The cottage belonged to seven dwarves. Every morning they left their cottage to dig for jewels and gold in the hills and every evening they returned home to eat and sleep.

When they returned home that night, at once they noticed they had a visitor.

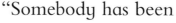

"Somebody has been eating my bread," said one.

"Somebody has been drinking my milk," said another.

"Somebody has been sleeping in my bed," said another. "Look, she's still here!"

Quickly, all the dwarves gathered round the bed to look at their sleeping visitor.

"Isn't she lovely?" said one.

"Let's leave her to sleep," said another. So, they left her until morning.

When Snow White awoke, the seven little dwarves were gathered around her bed. They were so kind that she told them her story.

The dwarves all agreed that Snow White should stay with them. Each day, when they went to dig for jewels and gold in the hills, Snow White stayed at home, cleaning and cooking.

Gradually, the years passed and Snow
White grew more and more beautiful.

Meanwhile the queen, thinking that Snow
White was dead, hadn't bothered looking in her
mirror. Then one day, she thought she felt a
spot growing on her chin and went to the
mirror to check. While she was there, she asked:

"Mirror, mirror, on the wall,

Who is the fairest of them all?"

You can just imagine her surprise, when it replied:

"In the dwarves' house, in yonder hill, Snow White is the fairest still."

The queen turned red with fury. Determined
to get rid of Snow White once and for
all, she began to plot straight away.

The following morning, the queen
dressed up as an old woman. Then
she filled a basket with pretty things
and went to the dwarves' cottage.

"Buy something from a
poor old woman," she cackled.
Of course, Snow White,
being such a kind-
hearted young girl, let
her in at once.

84

"Oh, these are ever so pretty," said Snow White, pulling some ribbons from the basket.

"Yes, just perfect for lacing your dress," agreed the old woman. Snow White let the old woman lace her dress with a colourful ribbon.

But the wicked queen pulled the ribbon so tight that Snow White fell to the ground. The wicked queen thought that she was dead.

When the seven dwarves arrived home, they rushed to Snow White's side and quickly untied the ribbon. Snow White gulped a huge breath and soon recovered.

"It must have been the wicked queen," decided the dwarves. "From now on you must always be on your guard. When we're away from home, you mustn't let anyone in."

Meanwhile, the queen had raced back to the castle and rushed to the mirror:

"Mirror, mirror, on the wall,

Who is the fairest of them all?"

And the mirror replied:

"In the dwarves' house,

in yonder hill,

Snow White is the fairest still."

The queen couldn't believe her ears. Once again, she began to plot.

In the morning, the queen called at the dwarves' house, dressed as a beggar woman with a basket of pretty combs – combs she had dipped in poison!

"I can't let you in," Snow White shouted from the window.

"Never mind," croaked the old woman. "Why don't you just try this pretty comb in your lovely hair?"

The comb was so pretty that Snow White leaned out of the window and allowed the old woman to push it into her hair. As soon as the comb touched Snow White's skin, she fell to the ground.

Luckily for Snow White, the seven dwarves came home early that day. When they saw her lying there, they guessed what had happened and removed the comb from her hair at once. Again, Snow White was quick to recover. Once again, the dwarves warned her about strangers.

The queen, meanwhile, was in a rage for she had just been told:

"In the dwarves' house, in yonder hill,
Snow White is the fairest still."

Now she was more determined than ever to destroy Snow White. So the next morning, she picked an apple that was half red and half green and injected poison into one half of it. Then, dressed as a farmer's wife, she called on Snow White.

"I just want to give you this juicy apple," smiled the farmer's wife, holding up the half red and half green apple. Look, it's not poisoned. I'll take a bite from it myself." And she took a bite from the half of the apple that wasn't poisoned.

Seeing that the apple did the farmer's wife no harm, Snow White accepted it and took a bite. But as soon as she did, she fell down as if dead.

That night, when the dwarves arrived home, there was nothing they could do to wake Snow White for, although she was not dead, she was in a very deep sleep – a sleep so deep that it seemed as though she would never wake.

Feeling very sad, the seven dwarves built her a glass coffin and placed her in the hills, where all who passed could admire her beauty for, although she slept for year after year, her beauty never changed. Her skin remained as white as snow, her hair was as black as a raven's wing and her lips were as red as cherries.

Then one day, a handsome prince saw the glass coffin and fell in love with the sleeping princess.

"You must let me take her back to my castle," said the prince. "I cannot live without seeing such beauty each day."

At first, the dwarves were reluctant to agree, but at length they saw that the prince loved Snow White and agreed to let him take her.

Very carefully, the seven dwarves lifted the glass coffin onto their shoulders and started down the hillside, but they stumbled and the piece of poisoned apple was shaken from Snow White's throat.

She awoke at once and on seeing the prince, she, too, fell in love.

It was a grand wedding. The whole kingdom was invited and all agreed that the bride was the fairest of them all.

Meanwhile, the wicked queen had discovered that her evil plan had failed. In her anger, she smashed her mirror and never looked at her reflection again.

Sophie in Toyland

Sophie was very sad. She couldn't find Peter the Panda anywhere. He was her favourite toy and she took him to bed every night. It wasn't long to bedtime and Sophie didn't know how she'd get to sleep without him.

Sophie sat on Beauty, her rocking horse, and rocked sadly backwards and forwards. As her eyes filled with tears, something – she didn't know what – made her rock faster than ever before. She closed her eyes. There was a tremendous whistling in her ears. The next minute, she was tumbling, head-over-heels, through the air, then floating gently down, to land on something soft.

Sophie blinked her eyes. Where was she, exactly?

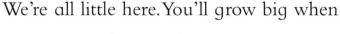

"Hello, Sophie," growled a voice
from above her head.

She opened her eyes and looked up.
The legs of a bed, her bed, towered above
her. It must have grown! Peeping over the edge
of her duvet was Big Ted. Next to him was Little Ted.

"Hello, Sophie," squeaked Little Ted.

Her teddies were talking!

Sophie looked around her. She was tiny!

"Help," she gulped, "I'm tiny! I've shrunk!" Her eyes filled
with tears.

"Hello, Sophie. Welcome to Toyland," called a voice from across the
room. It was Samantha, Sophie's doll.

"You're as tall as I am," gasped Sophie. "I'm no bigger than my
own doll! What's going on?"

"Don't cry," said Samantha, gently. "You're in Toyland, that's all.
We're all little here. You'll grow big when
Beauty takes you home again."

Sophie turned her head.
Beauty, now tiny, just like her,
was on the floor beside her.

"Mind out below!" cried Big Ted.

"We're coming down," squeaked Little Ted.

Big Ted tied one end of a cord to a bed knob and dropped the other end to the floor. It was the cord from Sophie's dressing gown! The bears climbed down it.

"Let's call the other toys," suggested Samantha. "Wake up, everybody!" she cried.

Suddenly, all of Sophie's toys sprang to life. Sophie's tiniest dolls dashed out of the dolls' house and the toys that had been put into the toy box jumped down from it.

"Let's play," suggested Big Ted.

"This is fun," said Sophie, as she played games with her toys.

All her dolls and all her teddy bears were there. All of them except Peter the Panda.

"Where's Peter?" asked Sophie, suddenly.

They looked everywhere. But Peter the Panda was nowhere to be found.

They gazed at each other in dismay. Then Sophie heard a soft noise. Everyone stood still and listened.

"Someone's calling," said the fairy doll, who had very good hearing.

"It's coming from the top of the bookshelf," said Sophie.

They crowded beneath the bookshelf. A tiny black and white head appeared over the top of it, high above them. It was Peter the Panda!

"I'm stuck," he squeaked, in a tiny voice.

"Oh dear," said Sophie, "I must have put you there when I was told to tidy my room."

"Please, get me down," begged Peter the Panda.

"But how?" asked Sophie. "The bookshelf is so high and we're so little."

"I know a way," said Big Ted. He dashed off and came back pushing Sophie's toy fire engine.

"We can use this," he panted.

"What a good idea!" cried Sophie. She turned the handle on the fire engine's side and the ladder on top got longer and longer.

It stretched higher and higher into
the air, just the way a real fire engine's
ladder does, until the very top of it
was resting against the bookshelf.

"Now, climb down, Peter,"
shouted Samantha.

"Ooooh, I couldn't possibly!"
said Peter.

"Don't worry," said Big Ted. "I'll get
him down." He climbed up the ladder and
lifted Peter onto his shoulders.

Everybody cheered and clapped when Big Ted carried Peter safely
to the ground.

"Well done!" said Sophie, hugging Big Ted and kissing his cheek.

Just then, the clock on the bedroom wall went "Cuckoo! Cuckoo!
Cuckoo! Cuckoo! Cuckoo! Cuckoo! Cuckoo!"

"Oh, dear," said Sophie. "It's nearly time for bed. I have to go.
Bye-bye toys, thank you for having me."

"Goodbye!" shouted the toys. "Please
come again!"

Sophie climbed onto the back of her
magic rocking horse and began to
rock. The next second she was back
in her bedroom, a big girl again.

Big Ted and Little Ted were slumped at the bottom of the bed. The fire engine, with Samantha the doll leaning against it, was down on the floor. The rest of the toys were all back in their normal places.

It seemed as though Sophie's adventure in Toyland had never happened, but the cord of her dressing gown was still dangling down the side of the bed, one end tied to the bed knob. Peter the Panda was lying safe on Sophie's pillow.

Lucky Sophie had been to Toyland! She'd had a great adventure with all her toys and she'd found Peter the Panda, too. Now she couldn't wait to go to bed and dream all about her wonderful adventure.

The Frog Prince

Once upon a time, in a land beyond the faraway hills, there lived a little princess. She lived alone with her father, the king. Although she was quite lovely, she was also rather spoilt because the king was a kind-hearted fellow, who allowed her to do whatever she pleased and he gave her whatever she wished.

She had so many toys that she couldn't possibly play with them all. But there was one toy she loved above all else – her golden ball.

One day, the little princess was playing with her golden ball beside an old well in the wood. She laughed and chuckled, as she tossed it into the air and caught it again.

Then, she threw it higher and higher, and, SPLASH, it fell down the well.

"Oh, no!" wailed the princess, as she peered into the deep, dark well. "I'll never get it back now. Oh, how I'd give anything to get my lovely golden ball back."

Then, as if by magic, an ugly frog appeared on the edge of the well. "What's wrong?" he croaked.

As you can imagine, the little princess was rather surprised to hear the frog talk.

"What did you say?" she asked, rather rudely, for she wasn't at all keen on green slimy frogs.

"I asked what was wrong," said the frog, very politely.

"Not that it's any of your business," said the princess, "but I've lost my golden ball down the well and I'd give anything in the kingdom to get it back."

"Anything?" asked the frog, with interest.

"Anything," replied the princess, rather grandly. "After all, I am the king's daughter. You name it. Jewels, money, land. Anything you want I could give you. But I don't suppose that a slimy old frog could get me my golden ball."

"Oh, but I can," said the frog. "And all I'd want in return is a promise that you will let me eat from your plate and sleep upon your pillow for three nights."

"Yes, of course," said the little princess, secretly crossing her fingers for she saw no reason for keeping a promise to a slimy frog.

So the frog jumped into the water and within minutes was back with the golden ball in his mouth.

"Hooray," cried the princess, snatching the ball and racing off before the frog had time for so much as a croak.

"Wait for me," called the frog. "Remember your promise." But it was no good. The spoilt little princess had already forgotten all about him.

That evening, the princess and the king were sitting down to dinner when there was a knock on the door. "Let me in, Princess," croaked a familiar voice. "Who is that?" asked the king. "Have you invited a friend to tea?"

Because she was always truthful to her father, the little princess told him what had happened by the well.

"Then you must let him in," insisted the king. "You have made a promise and promises must always be kept."

So, the princess opened the door and in hopped the frog. The little princess looked on in horror as the frog made his way across the room and hopped on to the table. "Hmm! This looks good," he said and began to eat from the princess's plate.

"Yuck! I'm not hungry any more," said the princess and she looked away so she didn't have to watch the slimy frog eating her lovely dinner.

When bedtime arrived, the princess tried to slip upstairs without her visitor. "Princess, I believe you've forgotten someone," called the king. So, the little princess had to come back and take the frog to her bedroom. She placed him on her pillow.

"Yuck!" said the princess, as she climbed into bed with her head close to the frog. She was certain that she would never be able to sleep with an ugly, slimy frog in her bed. Believe it or not though, in no time at all she was having a really lovely dream about a mysterious prince.

The following evening, the little princess once again shared her plate of food with the frog. This time, she even managed to eat a little herself and when bedtime came, she carried the frog to her bedroom and wished him goodnight before falling asleep.

On the third night, the frog came once more. This time, the princess even fed the frog from her golden spoon. Before going to sleep, she read the frog a lovely story. The princess was growing rather fond of the frog.

When the princess awoke in the morning she was surprised to find, instead of a frog, a handsome prince gazing down at her.

The prince explained how a wicked witch had changed him into a frog and sworn that he would remain a frog forever unless a princess allowed him to eat from her plate and sleep on her pillow.

When the king heard the story he was overjoyed that his daughter had kept her promise and broken the spell. He was even more delighted when the prince asked if he could marry the princess. As for the princess? Well, she was delighted that her frog had turned out to be a handsome prince and promised never to be a nasty, spoiled person ever again.

The princess and the frog prince got married and lived happily ever after.

The Golden Goose

Once upon a time, there was a woodcutter and his wife who lived with their three sons. The two oldest sons were clever and spoilt by their parents. But the youngest, who was called Dan, wasn't so clever or spoilt. Indeed, his mum, dad and brothers laughed at him.

One day, the woodcutter was unable to work in the forest, so he sent the eldest son in his place. His mother, who loved her eldest son dearly, packed him a fine lunch of sausage rolls and lemonade and waved him goodbye.

Before starting work, the eldest son, who was a lazy boy, thought it would be a good idea to have a little bite to eat. So he, sat down on a log and laid out the fine food his mother had packed him but, before he had time to bite the end of a sausage roll, an odd little man popped out of nowhere.

"Share your food with a hungry beggar?" asked the man, licking his lips and rubbing his hands together.

"Go away!" snapped the eldest son, who was mean as well as lazy. "This is my food and I'm not sharing it with anyone, especially a funny little thing like you."

"Well really," said the little man. "Nothing good will come from being so greedy and mean." Well, do you know, that's just what the eldest son found out for himself when, after finishing off all the sausage rolls and swigging all the lemonade, he cut himself badly and had to go straight home without any wood.

The following day, the middle son was sent to cut wood in his brother's place. Once again, his mother packed him a fine lunch. Once again, as he sat down to eat, the funny little man popped out of nowhere and asked for a nibble. Because the middle son was no kinder than his brother, the little man was again told to go away. Which was a mistake because the middle son also cut himself badly and had to go straight home without any wood. For you see, the little man was a magician.

On the third day, the woodcutter had no choice but to send his youngest son, Dan, to cut wood in the forest. This time, the mother couldn't be bothered to pack a fine lunch, for she considered that anything nice was wasted on her youngest and (in her opinion) silliest son. So, she gave him nothing more than a crust of stale bread and a bottle of sour milk and told him he was lucky to get anything at all.

On this occasion, when the little man popped up to ask for a bite to eat, Dan said, "I am afraid it is a very simple meal but you are more than welcome to share it with me. I always like making new friends."

So, you can imagine his surprise when he unwrapped the parcel of food to discover that the tiny scrap of stale bread and the bottle of sour milk had magically turned into scrummy sausage rolls and lemonade. Dan and the little man ate and drank until they could eat and drink no more.

"You've been fine company and I always say that one good turn deserves another," said the little man. "So why don't you cut down that old tree over there? I do believe you will find something interesting beneath it."

Dan chopped down the tree and do you know what he found beneath it? A goose with feathers of gold!

"Wow!" Dan exclaimed and turned to thank the little man. But he had vanished.

Dan knew that if he took the golden goose home his brothers would take it away from him, so, instead of going home, he decided to walk the world in search of his fortune.

After his first day's travelling, Dan found an inn where he could stay for the night. The innkeeper and his three daughters would have stolen the golden goose from Dan – but he never let it out of his sight, not for a single minute.

The next morning, Dan plucked a golden feather from the goose and paid for his lodgings with it. Then he tucked the goose under his arm and left. As the landlord's eldest daughter watched him walk down the road, she thought, "Hmm! Just one of those feathers of gold would buy me a very fine dress indeed." So she raced after Dan and reached

out to pluck a feather from the goose's tail. But, do you know, as soon as she touched the goose, she couldn't let go.

"Let me go! Let me go!" screamed the girl.

But Dan simply strode on, saying, "I can't stop now, I've got a whole world to explore."

So the girl screamed all the more, until her sisters came out to see what the commotion was about. They grabbed hold of their eldest sister and tried to pull her away. But as soon as they touched her, they, too, were stuck fast.

Dan strode on, ignoring the girls' cries. Then, as they were passing though the village, the parson saw what he thought were three girls chasing a boy. "Disgraceful behaviour!" he cried and caught hold of the girls to pull them away. But, as I am sure you have guessed, as soon as he touched the last girl in the line, he was stuck fast.

This continued until Dan and his goose had quite a following. There were the landlord's three daughters, the parson, a schoolteacher, a village blacksmith, a bellringer, four shopkeepers, thirteen housewives… Together they marched on and on until they reached a city where the king lived.

Dan had heard that the king had a daughter who, though very beautiful, was always sad and never laughed. This made the king so unhappy that he had promised her hand in marriage to whoever made her laugh.

Dan was used to making people laugh without even trying and so he was sure that he could bring a smile to the princess' face.

Boldly, he marched right up to the palace and into the courtyard. You should have seen how people pointed and laughed to see how Dan and his golden goose were followed so closely by such a long line of struggling people.

They laughed so much that the princess came to see what all the fuss was about. When she saw Dan and his goose, with the long tail of stumbling, struggling people following close behind him, her lips began to twitch, her chin began to wobble and, before she knew it, she was roaring with laughter. In fact, it wasn't a very ladylike laugh at all. But the king didn't mind one bit and he said that Dan and the princess should be married at once.

Dan never forgot the odd little man and when he eventually became king, he never forgot that "one good turn deserves another".

Little Red Riding Hood

Once upon a time, there was a little girl who lived with her mother in a tiny cottage on the edge of a large wood. The little girl's grandmother had made her a beautiful red cloak with a hood, so people called her Little Red Riding Hood.

One day, Little Red Riding Hood's mother asked her to take a basket of food to her grandmother who wasn't very well. She lived on the far side of the wood. It was a lovely day and Little Red Riding Hood always enjoyed visiting Granny, so she waved happily to her mother and skipped away.

Little Red Riding Hood hadn't
skipped very far when she stopped to pick
some flowers for her grandmother. Just
then a crafty-looking wolf wandered by.

"Hellooo, my lovely!" he smiled. "Where are
you going on this fine day?"

"I'm going to see Granny who lives in the
cottage on the other side of the wood," explained Little Red Riding
Hood, who had not been told never to speak to strangers. "She's not
very well, so I'm taking her this basket of food and a bunch of flowers."

"What a thoughtful girl," purred the wolf,
trying to hide his sly grin. "Well, I
must dash. See you!"

"Seems like a nice wolf, although he does appear to be in a bit of a rush," thought Little Red Riding Hood as she watched him race away. But then she forgot all about the wolf and skipped on through the woods.

Meanwhile, the wolf, who wasn't nice at all, ran all the way to

Little Red Riding Hood's grandmother's house. "Oh, goody," he smiled, as he peeped through the window and saw Granny lying in bed. "It's almost too easy." He licked his lips and rubbed his rumbling tummy.

"Yoo-hoo!" he called, as he knocked on the door.

"Is that you, Little Red Riding Hood?" croaked Granny, who had a sore throat. "Come in, the door's open. I've been expecting you."

With that, the wicked wolf pushed his way into the cottage and gobbled up Granny in a single gulp. Then, quick as a flash, he put on her spare nightdress and nightcap, popped on her glasses and jumped into her bed.

A few minutes later, when Little Red Riding Hood knocked on the door, the wolf pulled the blankets up to his chin. "Come in, my dear," he called, in his very best grandmother voice, "The door is open."

Little Red Riding Hood skipped into the house. "I've brought you some yummy food and…" Little Red Riding Hood stopped in her tracks when she caught sight of her grandmother.

"Oh dear, Granny, what big eyes you've got," she said, feeling just the tiniest bit afraid.

"All the better to see you with, my dear," replied the sneaky wolf.

"But Granny, what big ears you've got," she whispered, beginning to feel very afraid.

"All the better to hear you with, my dear," replied the wolf, trying not to snigger.

"And Granny, what big teeth you've got," she squeaked, now feeling absolutely terrified.

"All the better to EAT you with," roared the wolf, as he leapt from the bed.

Little Red Riding Hood managed one ear-piercing scream before the wolf pounced and gobbled her up in a single gulp.

Out in the forest, a passing woodcutter heard the loud scream and raced to see what was happening. He charged into the cottage where the greedy wolf was smacking his lips with glee. Quick as a flash, the woodcutter swung his axe and killed the wolf with a single blow. Then he drew out his knife and slit open the wolf's bulging belly.

Out popped Little Red Riding Hood and her grandmother. Granny was so pleased that she invited the woodcutter to tea.

From that day on, Little Red Riding Hood never talked to strangers again – particularly ones with big eyes, big ears and big teeth!

Harry's Gran the Pirate

Harry loved playing pirates! He would dress up in pirate's clothes and get his gran to chase him round and round the garden, while he shouted, "Shiver m' timbers!" at the top of his voice.

Gran loved playing with Harry but she couldn't help feeling just the tiniest bit embarrassed when people saw her pretending to be a pirate. After all, it just wasn't the sort of thing that grans usually did.

Gran and Harry were playing pirates one day, when the owner of Sandybay Water Park walked by. Harry and Gran turned bright red with embarrassment. They were sure that he was going to laugh at Gran for pretending to be a pirate. But they were wrong.

"Goodness me, you are a very good pirate," said the owner of Sandybay Water Park and he asked Gran if she would become a full-time pirate on the pretend pirate ship in the Water Park.

"Oh, I'm not sure," began Gran. But when she saw how excited Harry was, she quickly agreed.

From then on, she dressed up as a pirate every day and went to Sandybay Water Park to entertain children on the pirate ship.

Sometimes Harry went with her to help. At first, Gran was a bit embarrassed when she had to climb up the mast and shout, "Roll up! Roll up! Come and visit the best ever pirate ship."

But after a few days, she began to enjoy herself.

Children poured up to the lake to see the pirate
ship. They laughed at Harry's gran when she swished her
sword through the air. They laughed when she strode around the
ship's deck, roaring, "Yo, ho, ho, and a bottle of rum".

Harry thought it was great the way his gran made everyone
laugh and he laughed louder than anyone else.

But they all stopped laughing when some
big boys from Sandybay unfastened the ropes
tying the ship to the harbour wall and the pretend
pirate ship sailed out into the lake, taking Gran,
Harry and all the children with it.

"Stop! Stop!" cried the mums and dads
from the side of the lake.

"Help! Help!" shouted the children.

"Go on, Gran," said Harry, "take
the ship back to the harbour."

"But I don't know how!"
whispered Gran.

"Oh, Gran," said Harry, "you must do something!"
Of course, Gran wasn't really a pirate and she
didn't really know how to sail a pirate ship. So,
she handed out life-jackets instead.

Poor Gran. Poor Harry. Poor children. They all
ran round and round the deck, pulling this rope
and tugging that rope. But none of them knew
how to turn the ship round, or how to sail it
back to the harbour and so the ship continued to
sail on and on.

After a while, Gran was so puffed from all
the running about that she paused to catch her
breath. She looked over the ship's side. The
waves were very small, the lake was very
blue, the sun was shining and there
was hardly a cloud in the sky.

"You know," she
decided, "it's quite a nice
day for a sail."

The children looked over
the rail of the ship. "It is a nice
day for a sail!" they quickly agreed.

"Jib-booms and bobstays!" cried Gran. "Let's have a party."

All the children thought that was a brilliant idea.

"We'll have a picnic," said Gran. From the ship's kitchen she fetched one giant bag full of jam tarts and another bulging with sausage rolls. Gran made a big pot of tea. Harry made sandwiches with ham, cheese and tomatoes. One of the children wanted to hard-boil eggs from the ship's store-room, but Gran said the eggs had been on board so long that they were bound to be bad; so they put them back, taking care not to break them because bad eggs make a dreadful smell.

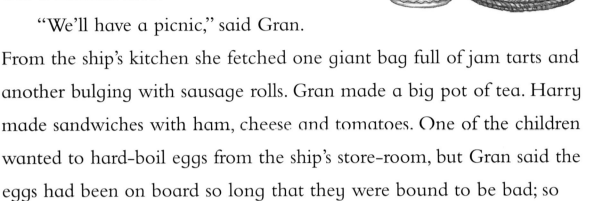

When the tea was made, and everything else was ready, they all sat cross-legged on deck and had a feast.

It was such a good one and everybody enjoyed themselves so much, that no one except Harry noticed the little ship was sailing into the bay of a sandy island.

"Gran," said Harry, "we've reached land."

"Land ahoy!" cried Gran, scrambling to her feet.

"There's a sandy beach," shouted the excited children.

"There'll be pirate's treasure, me hearties!" roared Gran.

"Excuse me, but there's another pirate ship over there," said one of the children.

Sure enough, anchored in the very same bay was another pirate ship, teaming with big boys dressed as pirates.

121

"It's the boys from Sandybay Sailing Club!" said Gran, "And they're all dressed as pirates."

"Yippee!" shouted the children. "We can have a real pirate fight!"

"They're hoisting the Jolly Roger," laughed Gran, as a skull and cross-bones flag rose to the top of the other pirate ship's mast.

"Prepare for battle!" cried the biggest boy from the other pirate ship, who you could tell was the captain because he wore a captain's hat, just like Gran's.

"They're going to attack us!" laughed a little girl.

The next moment, a bunch of slimy seaweed landed on the deck beside Harry's gran.

"Hooray! They're firing at us!" shouted Harry.

"Let's fire back," said one of the children. "If we don't do something fast we're going to be covered in seaweed and then we'll all stink."

"Stink!" cried Gran. "That's it, we'll make a stink! Children, fetch all the bad eggs from the ship's store-room."

When all the eggs had been gently laid on deck, Gran picked up the biggest and flung it at the big boys' pirate ship. It exploded on the deck in a splash of yellow yolk. "Bull's eye! Take that, you seadogs!" cried Gran.

"Poo!" one of the big boys cried out.

"Phaaaw, what a stink!" yelled another.

"Phew! Throwing bad eggs isn't fair," shouted the boy captain.

With their hankies over their mouths, all the children were soon throwing eggs onto the other pirate ship.

The smell became so bad that all of the boy pirates threw down their seaweed so that they could cover their noses.

"We give up, we give up," spluttered the boy captain who was gripping his nose so tightly that he sounded as though he had a bad cold. "Please let us come on board so that we can get away from this dreadful pong."

Gran allowed all the big boys to climb on board. Then she asked everyone what they should do with them.

"We could hang them all from the top of the mast," suggested one little boy in a quiet voice.

"Oh, no, they're far too heavy," laughed Gran.

"We could throw them to the sharks," suggested a little girl.

"There are no sharks around here," laughed the boys.

"Ummm, what shall we do, then?" asked Gran.

Harry stood on tiptoe to whisper in her ear.

"Well, I don't know," she said, peering down at him.

"Go on, Gran!" begged Harry.

"Oh, all right then," she finally agreed. She turned to the biggest boy. "Would you mind walking the gangplank?" she asked. "After all, that's a real pirate punishment."

The boy pirates thought that it sounded like an excellent idea.

So they blindfolded the boy captain and were about to make him walk the gangplank.

"Don't make me jump," giggled the boy captain, who really thought that it would be brilliant fun to jump into the lake.

"Oh, alright," said Gran, who didn't really think that making someone jump into the lake was a very nice thing to do. "But you must do something. After all, if I was a real pirate I'd make sure you were punished."

"Oh, please make me jump in,"
cried the boy captain.

But Gran wouldn't agree.

Suddenly, Harry had another
bright idea. He whispered in Gran's ear.

"What a great idea," cried Gran.
She turned to the boy captain. "You can
teach me how to sail, then I can take
the children back to the Water Park."

Of course the boy captain, who was really the captain of
Sandybay Sailing Club, quickly agreed. After all, if there was one thing
he loved better than pretending to be a
pirate, it was teaching people to sail.

Harry's gran was such a good
pirate that she learnt to sail in not
much longer than it takes a
pirate to flick his pigtail.

"Thank you," she
shouted to the big boys
as she steered out of
the bay.

A tremendous
panic had been
going on at Sandybay

Water Park ever since the
pretend pirate ship had
sailed away and as Gran
sailed into harbour a huge
crowd, including the park's
owner, was waiting.

As the owner frowned at
Gran and looked as if he was
going to say something cross, the
children all looked at each other and began to cheer.

"Three cheers for good old Harry's gran!" they cried. "Three
cheers for the best and bravest pirate ever to sail
the seven seas!"

"Hip, hip, hooray! Hip, hip, hooray!
Hip, hip, hooray!"

"Good old Gran!" shouted the owner
of Sandybay Water Park.

"Thank you for looking after our
children," shouted the mums and dads.

Harry was ever so proud of his gran.

"Shiver my timbers!" he declared,
"You're the best gran in the world."

"And you're the best grandson a
pirate could wish for," smiled Gran.

The Little Fir Tree

Deep in the forest grew a little fir tree. He was a very pretty fir tree, but he was not happy. He hated being so small and wished he was as tall as the trees who towered above him.

"Oh, if only I was tall, like you," he said to an oak. "Then I'd be able to look out over the world and birds would nest in my branches."

"Your time will come," said a friendly stork. "Why don't you enjoy being young? Just look how the sun warms you and the birds and animals play around you."

But the little fir tree refused to listen. Instead, he dreamt of things yet to come.

One day woodcutters came and cut down the tallest trees.

"Where are they going?" the little fir tree asked.

"Ah," squawked the stork. "I've seen trees like that sailing the seven seas, because they have been made into the masts of ships."

Well, the little fir tree thought being a mast and sailing the seven seas sounded far better than hanging out in a boring old forest. After that, he spent so much time dreaming of a life at sea that he barely noticed when summer turned to autumn, then autumn to winter.

Christmas drew near and men came to dig up the tallest fir trees and take them away.

"Where are they taking them?" the little fir tree asked the stork.

"Ah," squawked the stork. "They are taken into people's houses and decorated with balls and ribbons."

The little tree trembled with excitement. "Oh, that sounds even better than sailing the seven seas. That's what I want to do."

129

Another year passed and the little fir tree grew taller and stronger. Christmas came once more and men came to dig up trees.

"Pick me! Pick me!" cried the little fir tree. Of course, the men couldn't hear him, but because the little fir tree was so handsome he was the first to be dug up.

"Bye-bye," he shouted to his friends, as he was carted away.

Despite the bumpy road, the little fir tree enjoyed his ride into town. However, he was pleased when the cart pulled up outside a fine house and he was lifted off the cart. A man, a woman and two children came out of the house.

"Isn't it handsome," cried the woman.

"Isn't it tall," cried the man.

"Isn't it pretty," cried the children.

The little fir tree trembled with pride as he was taken into the house and stood in a wooden bucket.

"So this is my new home," he thought. "It's so much grander than the forest and my new friends say the nicest things."

The little fir tree thought he would burst with happiness when the children came and decorated him. When the man placed a gold star on his highest tip, he felt like the smartest little fir tree that had ever lived.

The following day was even better. First, the children sat around him to open their presents. Then, there was singing and dancing. Oh, how the little fir tree wished he could join in.

In the evening, the children sat around the little fir tree while their father told them wonderful stories. The little fir tree had never heard such tales. It really was the best day of his life.

Long after everyone had gone to bed, the fir tree shook with glee. He couldn't believe what an important little tree he was, nor could he wait to see what happened tomorrow.

Early next morning, the little fir tree stood ready for action. He waited and waited but nobody came. Then he heard footsteps and voices.

"We'd better get that tree out of here before it starts dropping needles," said the woman. "Come on, children. Let's take it out," said the man. They picked up the fir tree and carried it from the room.

"Let's put it in the shed," said the man.

It was very quiet and very dark in the shed. The little fir tree didn't like it one bit. He was left there for days and days and had nothing to do but think.

"I miss the forest," thought the fir tree. "I had so many lovely friends there. I wish I could go back there."

One day, the shed door swung open. The children had come in search of their sledges. "Hey, it's the Christmas tree," cried the little girl.

"Let's take it into the garden and plant it," said the little boy.

"What now?" thought the fir tree, as he was dragged from the shed and planted in the ground.

At first it felt cold to be outside once more, but as the sun warmed his trunk and birds rested in his branches the fir tree began to glow with happiness.

A large bird landed beside the fir tree. "So, this is where you got to. I've missed you." It was the stork.

The little fir tree trembled with excitement. This was the life – outside where a fir tree really belonged!

Puppy Love

Buster yawned, pushed past his brothers and sisters, and fell out of the basket. He trotted over to his bowl, helped himself to some water and waited for the other puppies to wake up. At the moment, they were still fast asleep. Four golden-haired little puppies that looked exactly like Ellie, their beautiful mother.

Ellie had given birth to nine puppies altogether. Sometimes they all wriggled up together in a big sleepy pile; at other times they chased around, nipping each other's ears and pretending to be big, fierce grown-up dogs. The other puppies loved to tease Buster, calling him 'Patch', but Buster didn't care, he loved being part of the golden-haired puppy gang.

After a few weeks, strangers began to visit

the house in search of
their dream puppy. All of them said how beautiful the
puppies were and nobody left the house without choosing
at least one of them.

Soon there were only five puppies left.

"I suppose," Bertie the cat remarked to Buster, "that you are
expecting somebody to take you away any day now?"

Buster stopped playing with his smallest sister and blinked. He
hadn't really thought about leaving home.

"Well, yes," he said at last. "I suppose so. Though
I'll be sad to leave Mum and the others, of course."

"I wouldn't worry too much about that," smirked
the cat. "I very much doubt whether anybody will
choose you anyway."

"Why not?" asked Buster.

"Take a look in the mirror," smiled
Bertie. "That should give you a clue."

Buster trotted over and looked in
the mirror. Staring out at him was a
little brown-and-white dog with a
patch over one round brown eye.

"Who's that?" asked Buster, puzzled.

"That's you, silly!" snorted Bertie.

"Me? But I look nothing like Mum and my brothers and sisters," he said in a small voice.

"Exactly," said Bertie.

"You're just special," said his mother, when Buster told her what Bertie had said. "Take no notice of Bertie."

But Buster knew that Bertie was right. Nobody would choose him.

That afternoon, a boy and a girl chose Buster's smallest sister.

"I suppose it's because I'm so pretty!" she said, waving goodbye to Buster.

"She's right!" hissed Bertie. "A funny-looking thing like you will never find a home."

Soon, there were just two puppies left.

"Time's running out," said Bertie. "It'll be the dog's home for you, at this rate. You can't stay here forever, you know."

When the doorbell rang the following morning, Buster barely bothered looking up from his basket.

"Pick me," barked Buster's brother. "See how cute and golden I am, not funny-looking like old 'Patch' here."

Buster sighed. He knew that his brother was right; nobody would want a puppy that looked like him. But, to Buster's surprise, when the door opened, two golden-haired girls made straight for him. One lifted him into the air.

"Look, Mummy!" she cried. "He's just like the puppy in Gemma's book. And look at his collar. He's even called Buster! We've got to choose him."

"He's perfect," smiled their mother. "Gemma will love him."

"Oh no she won't," thought Buster.

But Buster soon found himself driving away with his new family.

At last, the car stopped in front of a small red-brick house. Buster was picked up and taken inside. There was a lot of whispering and giggling, which Buster didn't understand at all, then he found himself being bundled into a small back room. "Oh, dear," thought Buster. "Is this the dog's home? Is this where I get left all on my own? He laid his head on his paws and waited.

Before long, the girls' father came into the
room. "Come on, boy," he said kindly, picking
Buster up. He tied a red ribbon around Buster's
neck and carried him to a bright, sunny room. The
mother and the two blonde girls were kneeling on the
floor among a small pile of presents. Sitting between them was a
smiley little girl that Buster hadn't seen before. She was younger than
the others, with an untidy mop of red hair, a freckly face and a pair of
round brown eyes. A little girl that looked nothing like her golden-
haired mother or sisters!

"Happy birthday, Gem," beamed the two blonde girls.

At the sight of Buster, Gemma sat down on the floor and smiled.
Buster threw himself into her arms and Gemma hugged him tight.

"Well," laughed her mother, "what do you think of him?"

Buster held his breath. Was she going
to say he was ugly? Was she
going to want to send him back
to his old house?

"He's perfect," Gemma
breathed. "He's exactly the
sort of puppy I've always
wanted. I'm going to call
him Buster, like the one in
my book!"

The Trouble with Finley

Finley was the friendliest gnome in the forest. He was never cross and he always had time for a smile and a joke with his friends. "Good luck," he'd cry whenever he saw George the gnome with his fishing rod. "Let me help," he'd say to Trixie Pixie whenever he saw her sprinkling morning dew.

So you can imagine everyone's surprise when, one morning, Finley was in a very bad mood.

"Good morning, Finley!" said Trixie Pixie.

"GOOD?" frowned Finley. "What's good about it?" Then he turned his back on Trixie Pixie. Trixie Pixie stared at Finley in amazement. Whatever was wrong with him?

He was usually so polite and friendly.

Just then, George the gnome puffed past on his way to the river. "Heard any good jokes lately, Finley?" he waved.

"You trying to fish – that's a joke," replied Finley, rudely. And with that, he marched indoors, slamming the door behind him.

"That's not like Finley!" gasped George. "I think we ought to find out what the problem is right away."

Later that morning, Trixie Pixie and George called a meeting to see if anyone knew what was making Finley so grumpy.

The air was filled with excited chattering, as pixies, gnomes, fairies and goblins tried to guess what was wrong.

"Perhaps Finley's got toothache," suggested Gobble. "That always makes me grumpy."

"Finley's got false teeth," replied George, "so it can't be that."

"Maybe he's hungry?" suggested Rosey Fairy. "I get cross when I'm hungry."

"Finley always has a big breakfast," said Trixie Pixie. "It must be something else."

Suddenly a voice piped up from the back of the crowd. "I know what's wrong!" said Pebble, who was one of the cleverest pixies in the forest. "He's not getting enough sleep. I heard him complain that the noise of the stream next to his house is keeping him awake at night. THAT'S why he's so grumpy."

"Pebble's right!" cried George, jiggling around in excitement. "I've heard Finley complain about the stream, too. But how can we put that right? We can't stop the stream from bubbling."

"I know what to do to help Finley get to sleep!" said Pebble. "All we need is a little bit of help from the animals in the forest! Now gather round and I'll tell you my plan."

"I do hope that stream doesn't keep me awake again," said Finley to himself, as he was getting ready for bed that night. "I really do need a good night's sleep for a change."

He was just about to jump into bed when suddenly he heard a loud noise outside his bedroom window.

TAP! TAP! TAP!

The noise got louder and louder and quicker and quicker.

TAP! TAP! TAP! TAP! TAP!

"What on earth…!" cried Finley, poking a very grumpy face out of the window. There, on a branch above his window perched a woodpecker, busily pecking a hole in the trunk. "Can't a fellow get any peace round here?" growled Finley, slamming shut the window and stuffing his hanky in his ears.

Finley folded back his bedcovers, filled his hot-water bottle and climbed into bed. But just as he was snuggling down under the covers he heard a buzzing noise. Bzzzzz! The noise got louder and louder, and closer and closer.

BZZZZZZZZZZZ!

Finley leapt out of bed and threw open the window again. There, hanging from the windowsill was a hive of bees, buzzing noisily.

"Really!" moaned Finley. "What a time of night to be making such a racket."

Finley turned off the light and snuggled down again. SCRAPE! Finley sat bolt upright in bed.

SCRAPE! SCRAPE! SCRAPE!

"NOW WHAT?" he shouted, marching across the room. He threw open the window and looked down. There, among the roots of the tree was a rabbit, digging a burrow.

"PLEASE let me get to sleep!" cried Finley, as he climbed back into bed and pulled his pillow over his head. But he could still hear TAP! TAP! TAP! BZZZ! BZZZ! BZZZ! SCRAPE! SCRAPE!

Just when Finley thought he would go mad, the noise suddenly stopped. All he could hear was the sound of the bubbling stream that flowed by the side of his home. After all the loud noises, it was like a gentle lullaby, singing the exhausted gnome to sleep.

Finley sighed a huge happy sigh. "At last!" he smiled, snuggling down under the bed covers. Before long, all that could be heard in the little house was the sound of the happy gnome's snores.

The next morning, it was a very different Finley who
met his friends at the garden gate. "Good morning!" he
cried, as George walked past with his fishing rod.
"Thank you," he chuckled, as Trixie Pixie skipped
past sprinkling dew. Finley was himself again!

"You seem happy today," said Pebble as

he strolled past

Finley's gate.

"I am!" agreed Finley,
smiling at the clever pixie. "It's amazing
what a good night's sleep can do for you. I slept
wonderfully well last night. You know, I think the noise of the stream
really is quite lovely!"

Pebble winked knowingly at the others. "I expect anything is better
than all the noise our helpers made," he grinned.

Anya and the Magic Carpet

Faraway, in a distant land, there was a sultan's grand palace, where many people lived. Among them was a small servant girl called Anya. Anya was a lovely girl, who worked very hard.

One day, Anya was collecting plates when she heard Cook calling her from the kitchen. As normal, she sounded very cross.

"Here I am, Cook," called Anya. "I was collecting the plates…"

"Well, hurry up then!" snapped Cook, snatching the tray from Anya. But as she grabbed it, the plates slid off and clattered to the floor.

"Now look what you've made me do!" Cook shouted. "Just get out from under my feet before you do any more harm!"

Anya ran from the room and disappeared up a flight of dusty stairs that led to an attic in the palace tower.

This was Anya's secret hiding place. No one bothered her here – not even the rats that gnawed at the carpets stored there.

Anya unrolled one of the carpets and sat down. Then, as she had done a thousand times before, she took the broken locket from around her neck and gazed at the woman in the picture inside. The smiling face always made her feel better.

This battered old locket was the only thing that Anya owned! For as long as she could remember, she had worked as a maid in the palace. Everyone told her she should be happy. "You could be out on the street like the other orphans," they said. But Anya didn't feel happy. She felt lonely and unloved.

"I wish I had someone to love me," she sighed, as a teardrop rolled down her cheek and landed with a plop on the floor.

Suddenly, the carpet beneath her gave a sharp jerk. Then it slid along the dusty attic floor, took off and floated in mid-air!

147

"A MAGIC carpet!" exclaimed Anya, in amazement. "I thought they only existed in fairytales!"

The carpet shivered as if to disagree, then began to fly madly round the room, zooming between the rafters.

"Whoa! Where are you taking me?" laughed Anya, as the magic carpet headed straight out of the open window, into the cool night air. It felt wonderful! Faster and faster the carpet flew, high above the city roof tops. Then, when the city was far behind them, it swooped down and hovered above a beautiful pool, where animals were taking a night-time drink. As the magic carpet moved slowly among the animals, Anya reached out to greet each one in turn.

The carpet landed beside a friendly deer and Anya hopped down and took a long drink from the pond. The water tasted lovely. Anya smiled around happily.

Then Anya climbed back on the carpet and they were off once more. Anya clung on tightly as they flew over mountains and seas. She'd never realised that the world outside the palace was quite so big.

Before long, they were in a town where Anya had never been before. The carpet swooped down and flew past the windows of grand houses. How Anya laughed to see the surprise on people's faces as they flew past.

Finally, the carpet landed with a thud on the river bank. "Phew!" gasped Anya. "That was a bumpy landing!"

"Who are you?" asked a voice.

Anya turned to see an old lady sitting on a bench by the river. The lady's face was kind, but Anya had never seen such sad-looking eyes.

"I'm Anya," she said, shyly. "I'm sorry I landed in your garden…"

But the old lady didn't seem to hear. She was too busy gazing up at the stars. Anya watched her face in silence. It was strange, but she felt they had met before – but that was impossible, wasn't it?

"I love stars, don't you?" said Anya, hoping to make the lady speak again. "Sometimes I wish on them!"

The woman smiled sadly. "I wish on them, too!" she sighed. "I wish that one day I will find my granddaughter!" A tear rolled down her cheek as she continued. "She was lost in a storm at sea. Her parents are dead now, but I have spent seven years searching for her."

"How terrible!" said Anya.

Just then, a moonbeam shone on the broken locket round Anya's neck. The old lady jumped to her feet and grasped the necklace in her hands. "Where did you get this?" she asked excitedly.

"I don't know," answered Anya. "I'm an orphan. I was found with it round my neck as a baby."

Trembling, the old lady reached inside her cloak and pulled out a broken locket, exactly like Anya's. With shaking hands, she pressed the two halves together. They fitted perfectly!

"What does it all mean?" gasped Anya.

"It means that you are my granddaughter!" cried the old lady, joyfully. "My daughter broke this locket in two when you were born.

She gave half to each of us. That is her picture inside."

"So now I really do have somebody to love me!" whispered Anya, in disbelief.

"You do!" replied the old lady, hugging Anya. "And now that I have found you, I will never let you go again!"

Just then, Anya felt a nudge behind her. It was the magic carpet. "You brought me here on purpose, didn't you!" cried Anya, happily.

"Thank you for making my wish come true!"

But the carpet just swayed gently before them, then swooped up through the trees and disappeared from sight.

"I wonder where it will go next?" smiled Anya, taking her grandmother's arm. "Off to make someone else's wish come true, I hope!"

151

Hansel and Gretel

Once, a long, long time ago, a poor woodcutter lived in the forest with his two children, Hansel and Gretel. The children's real mother had died a long time ago, so when the woodcutter took a new wife they were overjoyed. However, their joy was short-lived, for their new stepmother was a wicked woman who cared little for children.

One long winter, there was little food in the woodcutter's house and everybody went hungry. On one particularly cold night, Hansel and Gretel were so hungry that they could not sleep. As they lay tossing and turning in their beds they overheard their parents talking.

"There's just not enough food to go round," said the wicked stepmother. "Hansel and Gretel will have to go. Tomorrow you must lead them into the forest and leave them there."

"No!" gasped the woodcutter. But the wicked stepmother wouldn't leave him alone until he agreed.

"What shall we do? If we're left in the forest we're sure to be eaten by wild animals," sobbed Gretel.

Hansel sat gazing out of the window while he decided what could be done to save them. Then he noticed something that gave him an idea. The moon was shining on some white pebbles, making them stand out like daisies against a green lawn. Hansel crept down to the garden and collected a handful of the pebbles.

Early the following morning, Hansel and Gretel followed the woodcutter deep into the forest. As they walked along, Hansel kept stopping to drop white pebbles on the ground.

After a long walk, they reached a clearing in the middle of the forest. "Wait here," said their father. "I'm going to cut wood. I shall be back to fetch you at the end of the day."

Hansel and Gretel, waited and waited but their father never returned.

"We'll never find our own way home," said Gretel, as darkness began to fall. But Hansel told her not to worry.

When the moon eventually began to shine, the pebbles that Hansel had dropped stood out just as they had in the garden.

Holding hands, Hansel and Gretel followed
the trail of glistening pebbles all the way
home. Their father was overjoyed when
they walked into the house, but their
stepmother was far from pleased.

A few nights later, the children
overheard their stepmother talking once
more. "Those children really must go, or we
will all starve. Tomorrow you must take them even further into the
forest and this time make sure they can't find their way back."

After much argument, their father reluctantly agreed.

That night, Hansel tried to go out into the garden to collect
pebbles but his stepmother had locked the
door. So the following day, instead of
dropping pebbles, Hansel dropped
breadcrumbs on their journey
through the woods.

Once again, their father left
them and promised to return
before nightfall. Once again,
he failed to return.

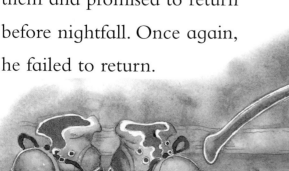

Hansel and Gretel waited for the moon to rise, then looked for the trail of breadcrumbs. But there was not a single breadcrumb to be seen, for hungry birds had gobbled them all up.

Hansel and Gretel wandered the forest all night long but they could not find their way home. Then, as the sun began to rise, they came across a pretty little cottage. Hansel and Gretel could not believe their eyes, for it was made of bread, cake and sweets. They were so hungry that they began to eat bits of the pretty cottage at once.

But before they had eaten more than a few mouthfuls, the cottage door swung open and an ugly old witch jumped out – a witch so wicked that she had built her delicious house to trap innocent children.

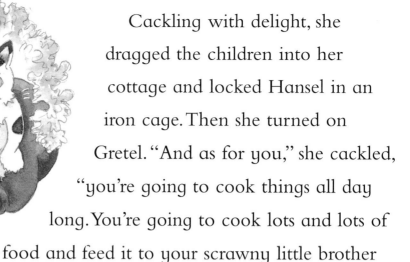

Cackling with delight, she dragged the children into her cottage and locked Hansel in an iron cage. Then she turned on Gretel. "And as for you," she cackled, "you're going to cook things all day long. You're going to cook lots and lots of food and feed it to your scrawny little brother until he is as round and fat as a juicy pig. Then I am going to eat him. And, if I am still hungry, I will eat you, too!"

From then on, Hansel was given lots and lots of the very finest food, while Gretel was given nothing but bones to gnaw on. One day, Gretel gave one of the bones to Hansel. "Hold it out to the witch when she asks to feel your finger in order to discover how fat you've become," said Gretel. "She is so short-sighted that she will never know the difference."

157

Clever little Gretel was right and the witch was astonished that Hansel did not get any fatter. Then, one day, she grew impatient:

"Fat or thin, I am going to eat him all the same," she cried. "Light the oven, Gretel. Today's the day we make boy pie."

Gretel did as she was told and soon the fire beneath the oven was blazing. "Is it hot enough yet?" asked the witch.

"I don't know," said Gretel, opening the oven door. "Why don't you look in and see for yourself?"

So the foolish witch stuck her head in the oven and Gretel pushed her in. Then, quick as a flash, she slammed the door shut.

Gretel found the witch's keys and released Hansel. Then they used the keys to open all the chests in the witch's cottage.

Inside they discovered all sorts of
precious jewels. "We will be able
to buy Father all the food we need
with this lot," laughed Hansel.

When their pockets were full with
jewels, they set off in search of their
home. This time, they found it without
much difficulty. When their father saw
them he was overjoyed that they had returned.
Quickly, they told each other what had happened. The woodcutter
explained that their wicked stepmother had gone and Hansel and
Gretel told their father all about the wicked witch and the jewels.

From that day on, the woodcutter, Hansel and Gretel never went
without food again.

Monkey Business

There was trouble in the jungle. Someone had stolen Big Baboon's prize melon and Lion was pretty sure he knew who it was. He decided to pay Monkey a visit.

When Monkey heard Lion coming, he tried to hide the melon behind his back. But the fruit was twice as wide as his skinny little body and it could be seen quite clearly poking out from either side.

Lion's brown eyes flashed with fury.

"Monkey," he roared, "this has got to stop! No animal steals from another animal in my part of the jungle. If you carry on like this, I'll banish you."

Monkey was cross and swung away through the jungle. As he did so, he saw Elephant trundling through the trees with a big pile of bananas on his back. The bananas looked ripe and delicious and Monkey's mouth watered. But Lion would be furious with him if he stole Elephant's bananas! He had no wish to be banished from the jungle, as Cheetah had been some months before for taking an antelope. What was a monkey to do?

As he wandered moodily along the river bank, a pair of eyes, a snout and two ears popped up from out of the water.

"Hello, Monkey," Hippo called in a friendly voice.

Monkey was in no mood for conversation. He ignored her and carried on his way.

"Ow!" he said suddenly, stubbing a toe on a hollow log that was sticking out of the water. He turned the log over in his hand. It reminded him of something. Of course! It looked exactly like Hippo! He slipped it over his head, gazed at his reflection in the water and chuckled.

He had just had a brilliant idea.

The next morning, when Hippo poked her head above the water, she found Elephant marching up and down the bank.

"Hippo!" trumpeted Elephant. "How dare you steal my bananas! The bush babies saw you sneaking away with them last night!"

"It wasn't me," protested Hippo. "I don't like bananas! Even if I did, my legs are much too short for me to reach the branches!"

But Elephant was in no mood to listen. He stomped off back into the jungle, crushing plants and bushes and making all the little animals skip hastily out of his way.

High up in the mango tree, with the hippo mask at his side, Monkey peeled a banana and chuckled softly to himself.

The next morning, Hippo had a visit from Lion. "Hippo!" he roared. "Crocodile's absolutely furious! Several of the night-animals have reported seeing you taking her eggs last night. One more stunt like that and you're banished from the jungle."

162

"It wasn't me!" protested Hippo. "I was asleep all night. Besides, I hate crocodile eggs!" she added, sulkily. But Lion had already stalked back into the bushes.

High up in the mango tree, Monkey cracked open an egg and chuckled to himself.

The next day, Lion called a meeting. "We have a problem," he told the animals, gravely. "Cheetah has returned to the jungle."

A murmur of fear spread through the crowd of animals.

"As you know," Lion continued, "nobody's safe when Cheetah's around. You will all have to be extra careful."

While Lion was speaking, Monkey dozed in his tree. His midnight raids had worn him out.

Later that night, Monkey put on his hippo log-mask and set off through the jungle. He chuckled when he spotted Ostrich fast asleep at the edge of the trees. Silly bird! She'd get quite a shock when she found her tail feathers missing in the morning!

As Monkey sneaked towards Ostrich, another animal prowled through the long grass from the opposite direction. The grass was so long that Monkey did not see Cheetah and Cheetah did not see Monkey until they were almost on top of each other.

As the two animals crashed into each other, Ostrich woke up with a great squawk, while Monkey let out a frightened little yelp. The little yelp echoed and rumbled inside the hollow mask, so that when it came out it had turned into a big, deep, booming ROOOOARRR!

It was all too much for Cheetah. While Monkey bounded back into the trees, Cheetah tucked her tail between her legs and fled, never to return to that part of the jungle.

The next day, the news spread like wildfire. Hippo had saved Ostrich and scared Cheetah away single-handed!

Lion led all the animals down to the river bank.
"Hippo!" he called. "Are you there?"

At the sight of the lion, zebra,
giraffe, snake, antelope and
elephant lined up along the bank, Hippo's heart
sank. She thought about diving down to the
bottom of the river bed and staying there, but
decided that she may as well get it over with.

"Yes, Lion," she said, in a small voice.

"Hippo," said Lion, "Ostrich has told us how you scared
Cheetah away last night. You are the bravest animal in the jungle."

"But Lion..." began Hippo.

"Not another word," said Lion, holding up his great paw.

All day long and late into the night, the animals sang
songs about Hippo's bravery and promised to bring her the
finest food the jungle had to offer every day for the
rest of her life.

Monkey stared down from his branch
high up in the mango tree. He didn't feel
like chuckling at all.

The Snow Queen

Once, there was a wicked magician who enjoyed making mischief. His worst ever bit of mischief was to make a magical mirror. This mirror was like no other, for it made everything reflected in it appear ugly. Beautiful fields looked like marshy swamps and the prettiest people looked like old hags.

The magician was so proud of his mirror that he flew with it round the world, causing trouble. One day, when he was flying high above the earth, he laughed so much over the misery his mirror caused that the mirror slipped from his hands and fell to the earth to splinter into a million pieces.

The splinters flew all over the place. Some stuck in people's hearts and made them cold and hard. Other tiny specks blew into people's eyes and made everything they saw appear twisted and ugly.

The largest piece of all fell on the Snow Queen, who ruled the icy lands of the north. From that moment on, she became the coldest and meanest woman who ever lived.

Meanwhile, far away from the Snow Queen's chilly home, lived a little boy and a little girl, called Kay and Gerda. Kay and Gerda were the best of friends and loved each other dearly. Every day they played together, even in the winter when the Snow Queen blew her icy breath across the land.

One winter's day, Kay and Gerda were making a snowman in the village square when Kay let out a cry.

"Ah! Something flew in my eye," he cried. "And I felt a pain in my heart." Alas, splinters from the magical mirror had fallen on Kay.

"Can I do anything?" asked Gerda.

"Get lost!" shouted Kay, before kicking over the snowman. When Gerda started to cry, Kay laughed. Then he grabbed his little sledge and sped away.

Kay played alone in the snow until a big sleigh stopped nearby. Kay could not see who was driving the sleigh but he did not care. He fastened his sledge to the back of the sleigh, so when it pulled away it took him with it.

On and on went the sleigh, dragging Kay behind it, until it reached an icy palace. Once there, the driver of the sleigh got down and called to Kay in an icy voice.

"Come here, Kay, you must be freezing." It was the Snow Queen.

Kay wasn't at all afraid. He wasn't even scared when the Snow Queen bent down and gave him an icy kiss on the cheek. The kiss cast a spell over Kay. It made him forget all about Gerda and think that the Snow Queen was the most perfect person he'd ever seen. But, worst of all, it froze his heart!

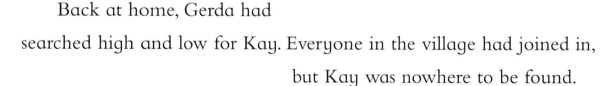

Back at home, Gerda had searched high and low for Kay. Everyone in the village had joined in, but Kay was nowhere to be found.

"Perhaps he has fallen in the river," an old man suggested.

Gerda took her best red shoes and threw them into the river, begging the river to give back Kay in return. But the river had not seen Kay and the red shoes were swept back.

169

"How will I find him?" wept Gerda. As if in answer, a little boat appeared at the river bank. Gerda climbed aboard the boat and was swept down the stream. On and on she went, through lands and kingdoms she'd never even known existed.

At last the boat came to a halt in a forest.

"Where am I?" Gerda asked a passing reindeer.

"Lapland," replied the reindeer.

"Have you seen a little boy with blond hair?" asked Gerda.

"I think such a boy is living with the Snow Queen in the North," said the reindeer. "Jump on my back and I'll help you in your search."

The reindeer galloped day and night until they reached the Snow Queen's palace. As Gerda stood outside the icy walls, she shivered with fear. But she knew that it was up to her to rescue Kay.

Inside the palace, Kay was cold and alone. The Snow Queen was away and all Kay had for entertainment were some chips of ice. The Snow Queen had told him that he could go home if he could form them into the word 'FREE!'. But, however hard Kay tried, he could not do it.

When Gerda saw her beloved friend, she rushed to his side. She held him in her arms and wept as she realised that he did not even recognise her. Her tears were so pure and full of love, that when they fell on Kay's chest they melted his frozen heart.

Kay began to cry too. As he cried the splinter of glass was washed from his eye. When he looked down at the chips of ice, they had arranged themselves into the word 'FREE!'.

Kay hugged Gerda with joy. "You're the best friend a boy could wish for," he smiled.

Their tears of sorrow were quickly replaced with tears of joy.

"Come on, let's go home," laughed Gerda. After that Kay and Gerda never fell out again.

The Wild Swans

There was once a king who had eleven handsome sons and a beautiful daughter called Elly.

Elly and her brothers couldn't have been happier. Their father loved them dearly and gave them everything they wished for.

Then one day, everything changed. The king took a new wife who was wicked and jealous. She was so jealous that she sent Elly to live far away and turned the eleven princes into wild swans and banished them from the kingdom.

The years passed and the king sent his wife to bring Elly home. The queen was furious when she saw the princess, for she had grown into a beautiful woman.

The wicked queen was determined that the king should not see Elly's beauty, so she rubbed dirt all over her face and hair.

When the king was presented with this ragamuffin, he would not believe that it was his beloved daughter. Poor Elly was thrown from the palace and the wicked queen cackled with glee.

Elly wandered day after day in search of her eleven brothers. The first person she saw was an old woman collecting wood in the forest.

"Have you seen eleven princes?" Elly asked.

"No, my pretty," replied the old woman. "But I did see eleven wild swans wearing golden crowns flying overhead."

Elly continued her search. One day, she came to a beach where she found eleven golden feathers.

"Surely this must be a sign," she thought, remembering the old woman's words. She decided to wait to see what happened.

Elly lay down on a bed of sand, until the sun began to set and she heard the flap of giant wings. Then, suddenly, eleven white swans landed on the seashore beside her.

Elly barely had time to admire their beauty before the sun sank below the horizon and the eleven swans were replaced by eleven handsome princes.

Elly and her eleven brothers were overjoyed to be together once more. Quickly, the brothers described what the wicked queen had done to them.

Elly listened to her brothers' tale; they were doomed to take the form of swans while the sun was up, but as soon as the sun set they became princes once more. This meant that every sunset they must be on land, otherwise they would fall from the sky and surely die.

Not only had the wicked queen done
this, but she had also banished them to
an island far across the great sea. They
were only allowed to return to their own
kingdom for eleven days each year. The journey they
had to make to and from the island was long and dangerous.
There was only one tiny island to stop at along the way, so the princes
had to make sure they reached this place before sunset. Otherwise they
would return to their human forms and drop from the sky and drown.

The eleven swan princes were due to return to their
island in the sea the very next day. Elly
begged to go with them, so they
stayed up all night weaving
a mat on which to
carry her.

The following
morning, as the
sun rose, the eleven
swan princes took off, carrying
Elly between them. The swans flew as fast as they could, but because
they were carrying Elly they were slower than normal.

As the sun began to slip beneath the horizon, Elly peered down at the sea and tried not to panic. If they did not reach the tiny island before the sun disappeared, the princes would return to their human form and they would all fall into the angry sea below.

Suddenly, Elly spotted a tiny dot below. As the swans circled down, the spot grew larger and larger, until an island appeared. Just as the sun disappeared, the eleven swans vanished and eleven princes and Elly thumped to the ground. They had made it only just in time.

The following morning, they continued their journey. At the end of a long day's flying, they reached their island home.

Elly was delighted with the cave they lived in. She spent each day alone and each evening was joined by her eleven brothers. However, she was not happy, for how could she be when her brothers were doomed to spend their days as swans?

Then one night, Elly had a
dream in which a fairy appeared.
She told Elly that if she made
eleven shirts out of stinging nettles
and threw them over the eleven wild
swans, the spell would be broken. But, she
added, Elly must not utter a word until the task was finished.

The following morning, Elly set to work. By the time her brothers
returned at sunset, she had finished one shirt. But her brothers were
worried. Elly's hands were raw from where the stinging nettles had
stung her, but she refused to tell them what she was doing.

Day after day, Elly worked on the shirts, until there was only one
still to make. She was picking the nettles for the final shirt,
when a trumpet sounded and a king rode by.

"What are you doing?" he asked.
But Elly could not reply.

When the king stared into
Elly's sad eyes, he knew
that he wanted
her for his
bride.

177

Thinking he was rescuing her, the king carried Elly off to his palace. His servants followed behind carrying Elly's belongings, including the nettles and shirts. At the palace, the king put Elly's things in a tower and gave her a key, so that she could go there at any time.

Shortly afterwards, the king married Elly and made her his queen. Elly began to enjoy her new life, but she was still determined to finish the shirts and break the spell over her brothers.

Early one morning, she slipped out of the palace and crept to the tower. Not realising that her husband was following her, she found the nettles and began making the final shirt.

The king, who was hiding in the shadows, was furious. He was sure that his wife must be a witch. He was just about to jump out and accuse her when he heard the flap of giant wings and eleven wild swans flew through the window.

He watched in amazement as Elly
finished her work and threw a shirt
over each of the swans. Then he let
out a gasp as the swans vanished and
were replaced by eleven princes. The
spell was broken.

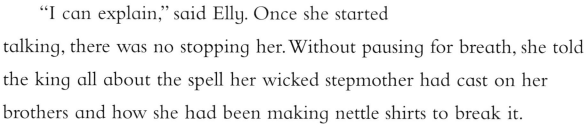

"What's all this?" cried the king,
stepping out of the shadows.

"I can explain," said Elly. Once she started
talking, there was no stopping her. Without pausing for breath, she told
the king all about the spell her wicked stepmother had cast on her
brothers and how she had been making nettle shirts to break it.

The king was delighted that Elly had
broken the evil spell over her brothers.

"You must all live with us in
the palace," he told the eleven
princes. And so they did,
until one by one they
each found a bride
of their own.

The Spring Unicorn

Far away, beyond the widest oceans, lies the enchanted land of Faria. The people of Faria are always happy, for the summers are long, the autumns are beautiful, the springs are a joy and the winters, although a little cold, are short.

It is such a beautiful place and the crops grow so well, that there is little for the Farian people to do but enjoy themselves in the sun. So they rarely work and, instead, spend their days playing, having parties, making music and telling each other wonderful stories.

Some people might say that they are lazy. But they wouldn't care because they are just so happy.

180

But one year it wasn't like that. That year, in fact, the people of Faria were far from happy. Indeed, they were very worried, for although spring should have arrived weeks ago – it hadn't. None of the winter snows had yet gone, the lakes had not thawed, the birds were not building their nests and the buds of the flowers in the mountain meadows had failed to open.

"It's not good enough!" said the king. "Something must be done."

He summoned the members of his Great Council to meet at the palace. "Whatever can be wrong?" he asked them. "What has happened to the spring?"

The men and women of the Great Council, except for one, shook their heads, for they did not know the answer. But the oldest and wisest member stood up.

181

"It is because the Spring Unicorn, the bringer of spring, has not visited Faria this year," he explained. "Without his arrival there can be no spring."

The king and the other members of the council looked at each other and frowned.

"But why has the Spring Unicorn not come to Faria?" asked the king. "Doesn't he like us any more?"

"I think it could be because we are so busy enjoying ourselves that we never thank the Spring Unicorn for all he does for us. It could be that he thinks we are lazy and don't deserve to live in such a wonderful place," suggested the wisest council member.

"But we must put that right at once," said the king. "All the people in all the land must leave the warmth of their homes and go out and start work immediately. They must start, ummmm, they must, ummmm…"

The king wanted to describe the sort of things his people should be doing when they went out to work – but the trouble was he knew nothing about work, so he didn't know what to say. In the end, he simply said, "Er…, they must, you know, they must bustle about being busy, doing work and things."

So, because the king told them to, the people of Faria went to work. At first, they didn't even know what to do. Then, when they'd looked up the word in the Faria dictionary and found out what was involved, they didn't like the sound of it and grumbled a lot among themselves.

But, as time passed, they discovered that they quite enjoyed being busy. They shovelled the snow from the paths of their gardens, they cleared snow from the roads, they repaired leaking roofs and even filled all the holes in the roads. They still laughed and sang, the way they used to before the spring failed to arrive and the king ordered that they should all go to work.

But it still kept on snowing, the lakes didn't thaw, the birds failed to build their nests and the flowers didn't bloom.

"What can the matter be, now?" asked the king of the oldest and wisest member of his council.

"Perhaps the Spring Unicorn doesn't know how hard we've been working," said the wise man.

"Well, the Spring Unicorn must be told," snapped the king, stamping his royal foot.

That very day, messengers were sent throughout the land to stick up posters announcing that whoever found the Spring Unicorn and explained how hard the Farians had been working, would receive all the gold they could wish for.

The problem was that nobody knew where the Spring Unicorn lived and so nobody felt brave enough to go out and seek him. Nobody, that was, except for a poor musician who was known as The Whistler.

"I'm fed up with winter and I've got nothing better to do, so I might just as well go and look for the Spring Unicorn," thought The Whistler.

So he picked up his flute and set off in search of the Spring Unicorn. He travelled far and wide, playing his flute to keep him cheerful on his journey. As he played, the notes of the flute danced before him, leading him on and on, across the widest oceans, over the highest mountains.

"I shall follow the notes of my music wherever they lead me," he told himself.

At long last, he came to a valley where no one had ever been before. It was the home of the Spring Unicorn.

"You have no place here," boomed a loud voice. "How did you, a mere Farian, find your way here?"

"I played my flute and followed the notes," explained The Whistler. Then he demonstrated with a quick tune.

His music was so beautiful that within minutes a whole herd of magical unicorns appeared and danced before him.

When he finally laid down his flute, one of the unicorns trotted forward. He introduced himself as the Spring Unicorn.

"Why are you here?" the Spring Unicorn asked.

"Because you failed to come to Faria this year," explained The Whistler.

"Ha!" cried the Spring Unicorn. "I couldn't be bothered to come because the people of Faria are so lazy they do not deserve my beautiful springs."

"But what you say is no longer true," explained The Whistler. "We are no longer lazy and we still have time to be happy, telling each other wonderful tales and playing beautiful music while we work."

With that, he picked up his flute again and began to play the sweetest tune the Spring Unicorn had ever heard.

"Maybe you are right," said the Spring Unicorn, when the tune had come to an end. "I'll tell you what I'll do. Providing you play your beautiful music on your journey back to Faria, then I shall accompany you and we will see if the people there are no longer lazy."

"Can I fly on your back?" asked The Whistler, hopefully.

"No," said the Spring Unicorn. "If we fly then the journey will be over too quickly and I won't have time to listen to all the music I want you to play. We shall walk back the way you came."

"Oh, bother," thought The Whistler, whose legs were really aching from all the miles he had walked on his journey to find the Spring Unicorn. Even so, he agreed to do as the Spring Unicorn asked.

So, The Whistler returned the way he had come and throughout his long journey he played the most beautiful music, so that the Spring Unicorn followed, every step of the way.

Eventually, they arrived in the mountains above Faria.

"Look," said The Whistler, pointing down to the village. "See how hard the people are working."

And, indeed, they were. Some were shovelling snow from their gardens – but as soon as they had finished, more snow fell to replace it. Some were clearing snow from the roads – but as soon as they stood up to rest their backs, more snow was covering them over. Some were mending leaks in their roofs – but as soon as they had finished, more snow was falling to make new holes.

"Indeed, they are working," admitted the Spring Unicorn. "But are they happy in their work?"

"Listen," said The Whistler.

The Unicorn listened. Faintly, from the village, came the sound of someone laughing. Someone else was whistling. Someone else was singing.

"Oh, yes," said The Whistler. "I think you can say they are happy."

"I believe you're right," agreed the Unicorn. "You shall have your spring back again and I shall continue to bring a new spring, year after year, just so long as the people remain happy and contented and do not ever become lazy again."

That's how it was. And that's how it still is. Spring comes every year to Faria and the people remain happy and contented. They work harder now than they did before, but never too hard. There is still time for them to party and make music and tell each other stories.

As for The Whistler? Well, he turned down the king's offer of riches in favour of becoming the Spring Unicorn's helper. Which is why, every year, the Farian spring is always heralded by the most beautiful music anyone has ever heard.